ADAM GILCHRIST'S
CHAMPIONS of CRICKET

illustrated by **MICHAEL WELDON**

books that leave an impression

First published by Affirm Press, 2021
28 Thistlethwaite Street, South Melbourne,
Boonwurrung Country, VIC 3205
1 3 5 7 9 10 8 6 4 2
Text copyright © Adam Gilchrist, 2021
Illustrations copyright © Michael Weldon, 2021
The moral rights of the author and illustrator have been asserted.
All rights reserved. No part of this publication may be reproduced without the prior permission of the publisher.

 A catalogue record for this book is available from the National Library of Australia

ISBN: 9781922626127 (hardback)
Cover and internal design © Affirm Press
Printed and bound in China by RR Donnelley Asia Printing Solutions Ltd.

affirmpress.com.au

CONTENTS

Introduction iv
Cricket Map vi

Belinda Clark 2
David Warner 6
Justin Langer 10
Ricky Ponting 14
Dean Jones 18
Meg Lanning 22
Usman Khawaja 26
Allan Border 30
Steve Smith 34
Chris Lynn 38
Glenn Maxwell 42
Marnus Labuschagne 46
Beth Mooney 50
Tim Paine 54
Alyssa Healy 58

Pat Cummins 62
Dennis Lillee 66
Josh Hazlewood 70
Glenn McGrath 74
Shane Warne 78
Fawad Ahmed 82
Nathan Lyon 86
Ashton Agar 90
Ashleigh Gardner 94
Steve Waugh 98
Alex Blackwell 102
Mitch Marsh 106
Andrew Symonds 110
Ellyse Perry 114
Cameron Green 118

Adam Gilchrist 122

INTRODUCTION

DREAMS TO REALITY

I have such happy memories of playing backyard cricket as a kid. Growing up in country New South Wales, far from the ocean, we did play beach cricket, but it was on the sand of the river that ran through town. My siblings and I were always looking for the straightest sticks to use as stumps. The whole family and often our neighbours got involved. I am the youngest of four kids so I did a lot of chasing of the ball and a lot of bowling because I couldn't get a bat. Wherever we could play, it was always on. I remember watching Dennis Lillee and noticing that after a few overs, his footprints were visible in the grass. I tried to do the same thing in the backyard (sorry, Dad!). A few windows were broken. Many balls were lost over fences or on the roof. I cut my hand trying to climb the corrugated iron fence to get balls back. The game simply had to go on.

I remember watching my childhood cricketing heroes, many of whom I talk about in this book, and thinking they couldn't be real. They were on TV and they were amazing. I never really thought I would be able to do what they did and be a professional cricketer. Well, at least not until my dad took me to the Sydney Cricket Ground when I was nine years old. I was mesmerised. It was like what I had seen on TV, but it was real and there was so much more to look at than what the camera showed. And seeing the players made me realise they were human. I loved the game already before this moment, but this experience made me think I wanted to be a cricketer and that maybe, just maybe, if I worked hard and was lucky, I might get to be.

I didn't get off to the best start wicketkeeping though. I broke my nose the first time I tried it when I was 10 years old. I was filling in for my older brother's team, and they had stuck me behind the stumps – probably to keep me out of the way, but I was keen to do it. The ball came in, hit the edge of the cement pitch and came up and broke my nose. I spent the night in hospital feeling pretty down and out. That night, a nurse at the hospital told me that Rod Marsh broke his nose the first time he wicketkept. That really lifted my spirits. I remember thinking this might be fate. Many years later when I met Rod Marsh, I asked him about it and he said he had never broken his nose. I'm not sure where the nurse got that story from but it helped me feel better at the time, and it might have set me on my cricketing career.

When I became a professional cricketer, I had two superstitions – or a better word might be routines – that I always tried to follow. I always stepped onto the field with my left foot first. It gave me confidence and made me feel safe. I never stepped onto the field with my right foot! And, if it was possible, the night before a Test match (and I played 96 of them!), I always ate penne arrabbiata. It was my lucky dinner. Those two things were my rituals. They helped me mentally prepare for what was about to happen on the field.

The players in this book are a blend of my childhood heroes, the legends I got to play the great game with and the players that inspire me today. Together, these players reflect the journey of cricket from past to present They show how the game has changed over time and become the sport we watch today. All the players in this book demonstrate that they are, or were, committed to their team – something that is so important to me. Cricket is the most individual of team sports. But I can tell you that getting a positive personal result in a losing team is a hollow feeling. The only true success comes as a team. I've really enjoyed learning their stories and watching their cricket and I hope you do, too.

Adam Gilchrist

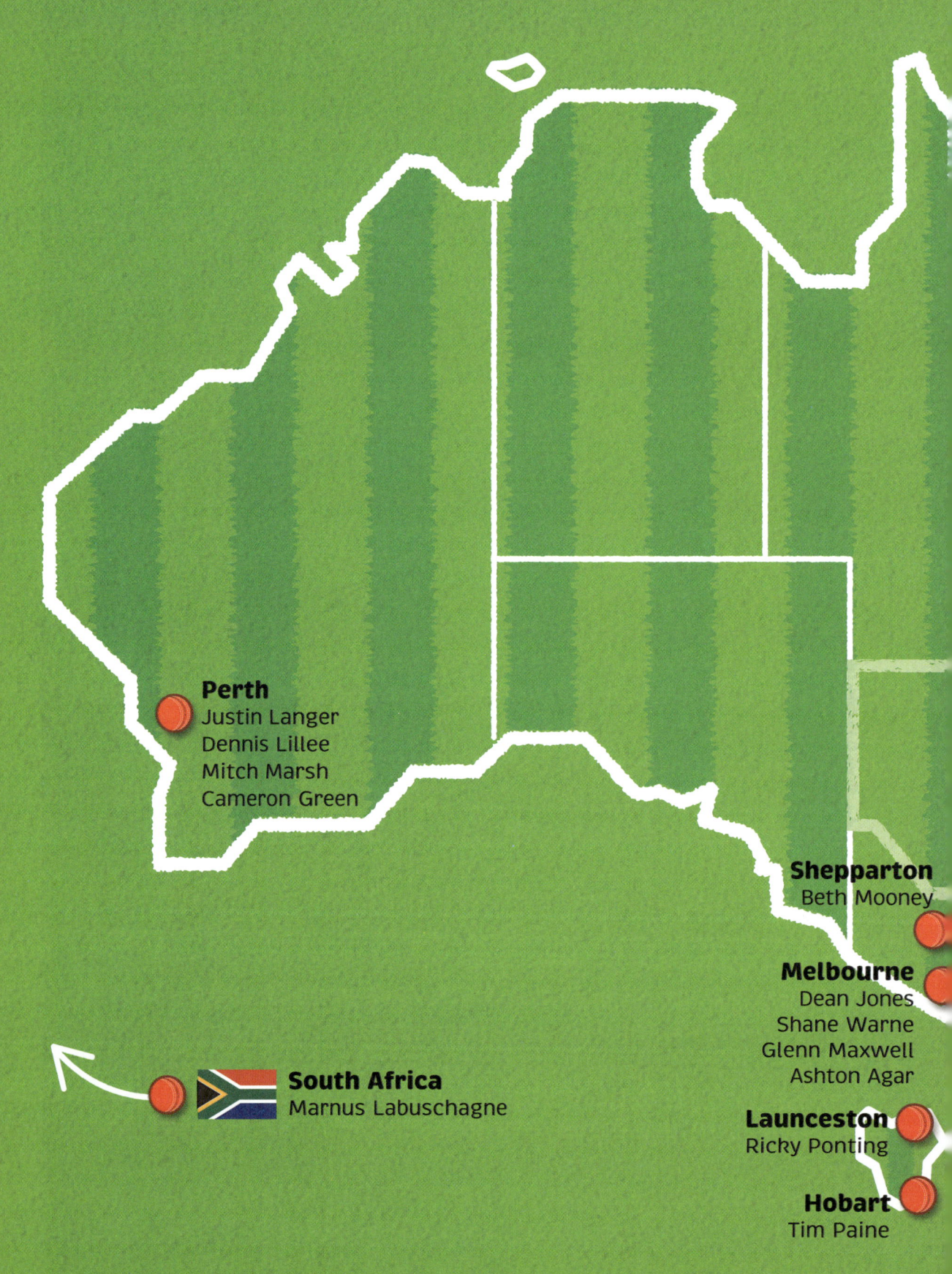

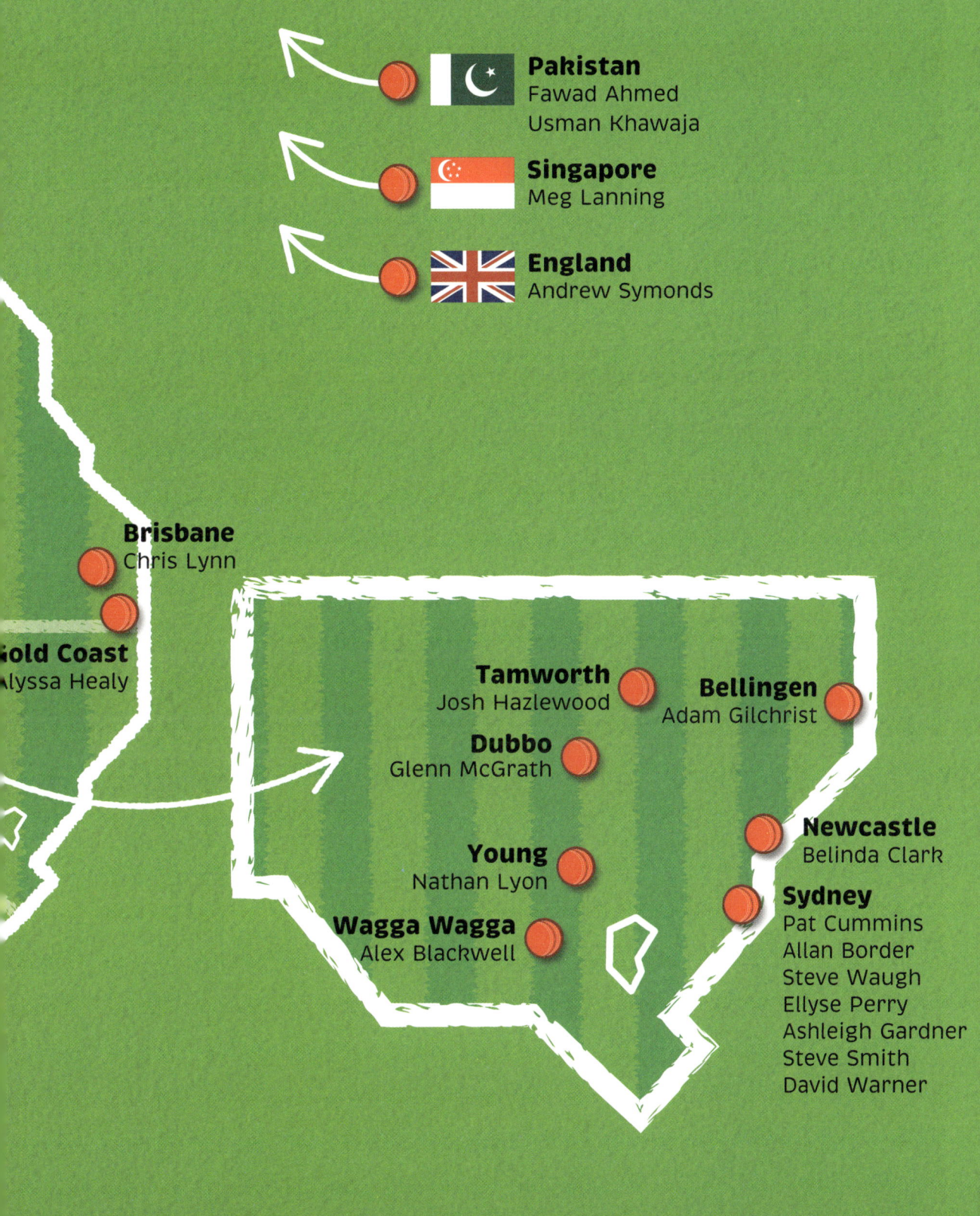

BELINDA CLARK

Belinda Clark has done more for Australian women's cricket than almost anybody else. She is an icon and legend of the game.

GILLY SAYS

**BORN 10 SEPTEMBER 1970
NEWCASTLE, NEW SOUTH WALES**

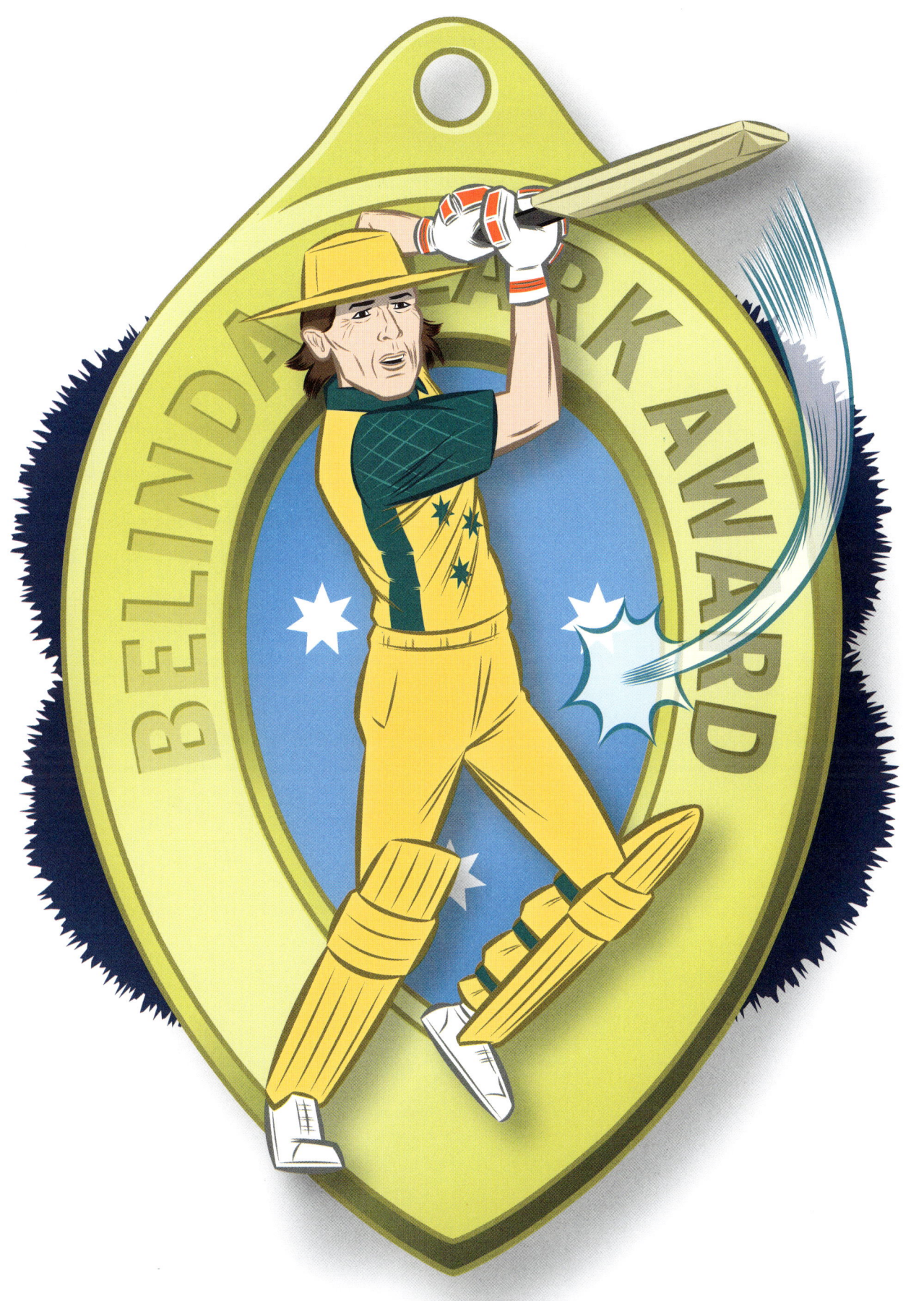

BELINDA CLARK

RIGHT-HANDED OPENING BATTER

Belinda Clark played for the Australian women's national team from 1991 to 2005 and captained it from 1994 to 2005. The way she played the game is legendary. She set the standard for women's cricket. Thanks to her, the Australian women's team were dominant against all opposition around the world for a significant amount of time.

Belinda was a skilled master of cricket. Many of her records and stats rivalled those of male players at the time. That hadn't happened before Belinda. She made statements with her bat, and her results and dominance speaks for itself. Cricket may traditionally have been a game played by men but Belinda completely changed that and Australian women's cricket never looked back.

Belinda broke through all kinds of barriers to make people pay attention to the skilled, talented young women playing cricket who were executing their skills on the global stage to the highest level. And they were doing so while all of them had to work as they were not being paid to play. If we look at the women's game before Belinda Clark, players had to pay to go to World Cups and represent their country! Belinda pioneered the women's game both in terms of inspiring young players to follow in her footsteps and also ensuring that the game was administered properly and players received proper payment. She had to overcome so much more compared to the male players of her day, including me. What she managed to achieve in all aspects of the sport is awe-inspiring.

Clark was the first batter to score a double century in a One Day International when she scored 229 against Denmark in the 1997 World Cup. Not just the first female player: the first player. It was the holy grail of men's One Day cricket and nobody achieved it before Clark. Everybody was trying to achieve that goal. The first male player to reach that milestone was India's Sachin Tendulkar who managed it 13 years after Clark.

Clark loves cricket and has many wonderful ideas about the sport. She has left a strong legacy on the game for all players, and she's still heavily invested in the game and is a key part of the direction of the sport. The highest honour in women's cricket today is receiving the Belinda Clark Award. Current players look up to her and admire her so much, and that's obvious to everyone in the sport. It is so fitting that this honour is named after Belinda.

PLAYING CAREER

CAREER: 1991–2005 Test & ODI
MATCHES: 15 Test, 118 ODI
RUNS: 919 Test runs, 4,844 ODI runs
CENTURIES & FIFTIES: 2 & 6 Test, 5 & 30 ODI
BATTING AVERAGE: 45.95 Test, 47.49 ODI
HIGH SCORE: 136 Test, 229* ODI
FIELDING: 4 Test dismissals (4 Ct), 45 ODI dismissals (45 Ct)

DAVID WARNER

This guy came out of nowhere to play for Australia in 2009. And since then he's been an integral part of the Australian batting line-up.

**BORN 27 OCTOBER 1986
PADDINGTON, NEW SOUTH WALES**

DAVID WARNER

LEFT-HANDED OPENING BATTER

David Warner played cricket for Australia before he had even played Sheffield Shield cricket for New South Wales. Suddenly there he was on the MCG scoring 89 against a South African bowling line-up that was world-class and dominating. It was entertaining, and I thought this guy's going to be good fun to watch in white-ball – short version – cricket.

Like many people, I had doubts about Warner's capability in Test cricket. I made a judgement call that he didn't have the technique for it. But I was so happy to be proven wrong about this. Warner developed and perfected a very aggressive batting approach. It can be risky to bat aggressively rather than defensively, but it's Warner's way and I wouldn't have him do anything differently. Warner made a memorable 180 runs in the third Test against India in Perth in 2012, before a scorching century against South Africa in Adelaide the following summer. Along with Steve Smith, he has been such an important part of Australia's batting line-up in all three formats of the game.

Warner bats to his strengths. His style is sound – he does not have a textbook perfect style but neither is it erratic and risky. It's about controlled aggression. Warner knows the areas he can be dominant in a game. It's almost a game of patience: he waits for when the bowler is getting tired or maybe even bored and decides to try something new, and that is the moment Warner swoops in and takes control of the innings. He is very quick to pounce on any opening and takes advantage of any error a bowler might make.

Warner can play all the strokes and he can play hook shots and cut shots really well. Being a bit shorter means the ball bounces a bit more, so these shots are particularly important. As soon as a bowler over-pitches into Warner's area, he gets on the front foot and drives the ball really aggressively. But as much as anything in his batting skill set, Warner's game style allows him to put pressure on bowlers straight away. They know that he's going to be aggressive and attack every ball. That can draw error from a bowler. It's all about mindset. As soon as you start worrying about how to bowl, you often make the mistake you're telling yourself in your mind not to make. Warner is very good at mind victories.

Warner proved me wrong early in his career, and he continues to do so. We need to keep open minds when judging technique – people can and will surprise you.

PLAYING CAREER

*as of 18 July, 2021

CAREER: 2011-present Test, 2009-present ODI & T20I

MATCHES: 86 Test, 128 ODI, 81 T20I

RUNS: 7,311 Test runs, 5,455 ODI runs, 2,265 T20I runs

CENTURIES & FIFTIES: 24 & 30 Test, 18 & 23 ODI, 1 & 18 T20I

BATTING AVERAGE: 48.09 Test, 45.45 ODI, 31.45 T20I

HIGH SCORE: 335* Test, 179 ODI, 100* T20I

KEEPING: 69 Test dismissals (69 Ct), 56 ODI dismissals (56 Ct), 44 T20I dismissals (44 Ct)

JUSTIN LANGER

Langer is the most honest and loyal man I know. He is a man of integrity. I admire him so much as a cricketer and a leader.

GILLY SAYS

**BORN 21 NOVEMBER 1970
PERTH, WESTERN AUSTRALIA**

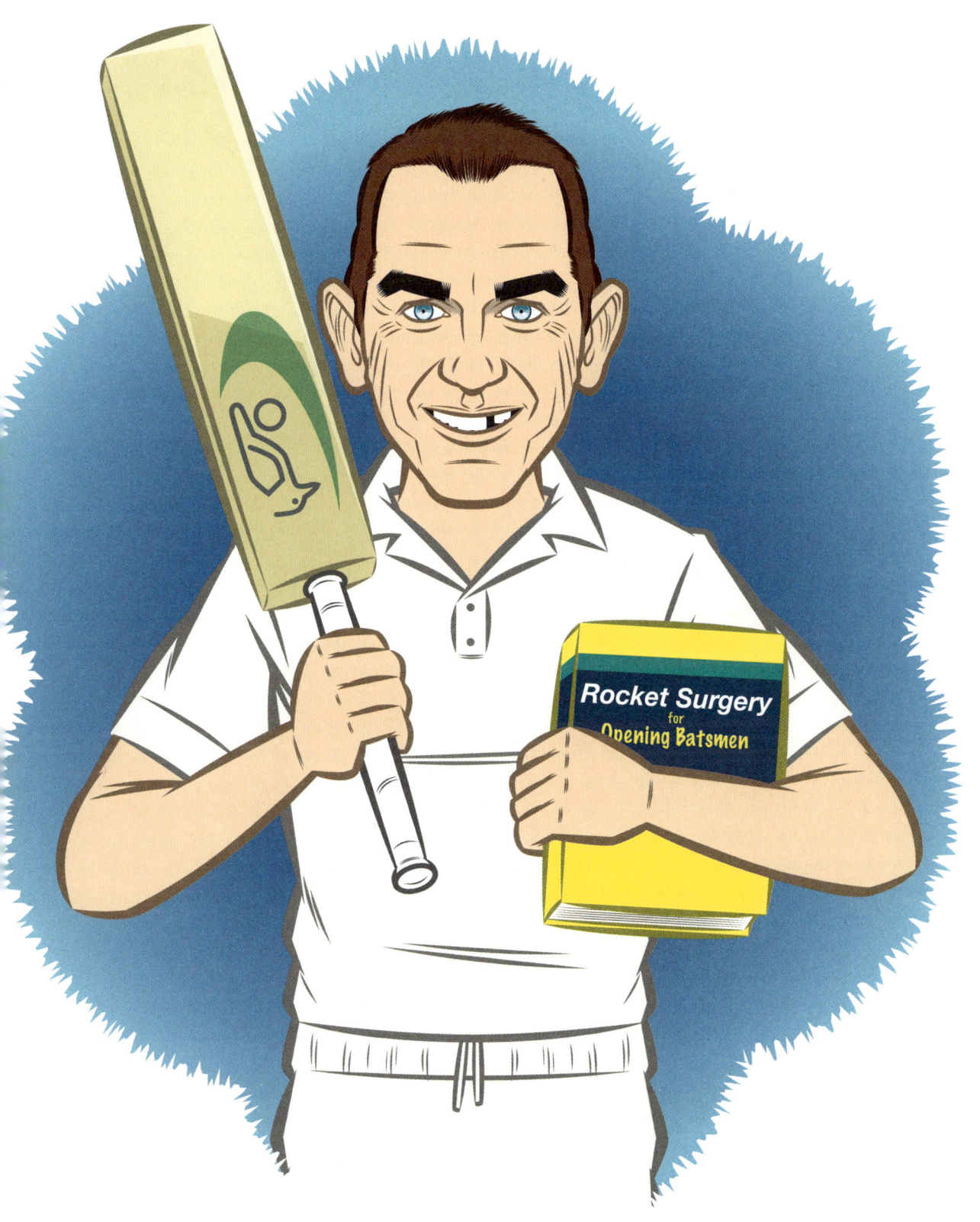

JUSTIN LANGER

LEFT-HANDED OPENING BATTER

Contemporaries of Justin Langer's from underage cricket might be surprised he ended up where he did. He had cricket heritage in his family with his uncle Robbie playing for Australia, but nothing came particularly naturally to Justin in the way it might have to a number of other players around him. At that age, Ricky Ponting and Damien Martyn were a step above everybody, and people might have underestimated Langer's potential. But Justin was one of the hardest workers I have ever known. He was so determined. Justin believes there is nothing a batter cannot teach themselves, and he worked hard to make the most of his talents. You may not be the best hitter, but Langer shows that you can build your skills with hard work and perseverance.

People like Langer are very good at seeing opportunities. He approaches life with his eyes wide open and makes the most of everything that comes his way. A breakthrough opportunity came for Justin when he was 21. A player got injured and Langer was called up the day before to play in the Sheffield Shield final. He scored 149 in that final and thinks of it as his best innings.

One of my favourite moments playing with Justin came early in my international career. It was my second Test and we were playing in Hobart in 1999. Shoaib Akhtar, the fastest bowler in the world at that time, bowled a bouncer and it hit Langer in the grille of the helmet. I ran down to see if he was all right. Justin looked up at me and had the biggest smile on his face. He looked at me and said, 'This is the best. This is what it's all about.' His love of the game shone through. He is so passionate about cricket, and particularly Australian cricket.

Langer is a terrific coach. He's continuing to learn and is always trying to improve. Justin was always at the front of the pack in training, but coaching has shown him that not everyone can be at the front. He has learnt how to help bring people closer to the front and lift their level. And importantly, he cares about his players. He sets very achievable and sustainable standards based on trust, loyalty and honesty. He's a legend.

Justin is a great observer of life and a big reader. He loves quotes and he has a room in his house with a wall that's covered in them. My favourite is something that Steve Waugh would often say: 'Attitudes are contagious. Is yours worth catching?' I think it's a great question to ask yourself every day, and it sums up Justin's approach to cricket and life.

PLAYING CAREER

CAREER: 1993–2007 Test, 1994–1997 ODI
MATCHES: 105 Tests, 360 First Class
RUNS: 7,696 Test runs, 28,382 First Class runs
CENTURIES & FIFTIES: 23 & 30 Test, 86 & 110 First Class
BATTING AVERAGE: 45.27 Test, 50.23 First Class
HIGH SCORE: 250 Test, 342 First Class
FIELDING: 73 Test dismissals (73 Ct), 3 ODI dismissals (2 Ct, 1 St)

RICKY PONTING

Ricky is simply one of the greatest cricketers of all time and was a great captain. He led by example but also seemed to know exactly what to say to get the best out of each team member.

GILLY SAYS

**BORN 19 DECEMBER 1974
LAUNCESTON, TASMANIA**

RICKY PONTING
RIGHT-HANDED TOP ORDER BATTER

Ricky Ponting's destiny to become a cricketing legend was pretty obvious from a young age. He scored four centuries for the Under-13s in a cricket week! He then went on to score two more when he was pushed up to the Under-16 team. He was always playing in older age group categories and didn't spend a lot of time in the youngsters playing with his peers. He was a little scrapper from Launceston, but the expectations and pressure from such a young age never seemed to get in his way. By the time he was 20, he was playing Test cricket. He had a fierce determination.

When I think of Ricky Ponting, I immediately recall him scoring 140 not out in the World Cup Final in Johannesburg in 2003. It was a symbolic moment that says so much about his cricketing career. His dominance in that match, which was the biggest match on the biggest stage in the cricketing world at that point in time, showed what a truly magnificent batter he was. It symbolised his position in global cricket: he was the leader of a team that had just won a World Cup for the second time in a row and that had been undefeated in that tournament. And it showed who he was as a leader. He was so highly respected and supported by his team and Australian cricket in general.

As a captain, Ricky led by example. He had the clear intention to improve at whatever he was doing. His ability to look for improvements, whether it was skills or techniques or fitness, was second to none. He also worked at how best to communicate with each and every player. The way that he led by example was like Steve Waugh before him, but he also learnt to communicate with each player like Mark Taylor.

A side of Ricky that not many people know about is how funny he is. I first met him when he was 17 and we toured to South Africa with the Australian Institute of Sport team. He was such a prankster! He would hide someone's bat just when they were walking out to bat. In 1998 at the Commonwealth Games, he booby trapped the rooms so water fell on your head when you walked in, or he put things there to trip you over. That type of humour is Ricky to a tee – he was like a pesky little brother.

It's all well and good to have a captain who is a wonderful player in their own right and a great leader, but what meant most to me was Ricky's trust in me. Being his vice-captain was a role I took seriously. I felt his complete trust in me as a cricketer, as a batter and as a vice-captain. Ponting brought out the best in everyone around him.

PLAYING CAREER

CAREER: 1995–2012 Test & ODI
MATCHES: 168 Tests, 375 ODIs
RUNS: 13,378 Test runs | 13,704 ODI runs
CENTURIES & FIFTIES: 41 & 62 Test, 30 & 82 ODI
BATTING AVERAGE: 51.85 Test, 42.03 ODI
HIGH SCORE: 257 Test, 164 ODI
FIELDING: 196 Test dismissals (196 Ct), 160 ODI dismissals (160 Ct)

DEAN JONES

> Dean Jones is an absolute idol of mine. I grew up observing him and wanting to be him. Everything about him looked cool, fun and aggressive. Such fun to watch.

GILLY SAYS

**BORN 24 MARCH 1961
COBURG, VICTORIA**

DEAN JONES

RIGHT-HANDED TOP ORDER BATTER

Dean Jones really showed the world how to play One Day cricket both as a batter and as a fielder. And that was on the back of a very decent Test career! I'll never forget when he played a Test against India in 1986 – he was sick with gastro but battled on and scored an amazing double century.

Dean's One Day feats were just mesmerising. Everything about the One Day format suited him: the lights, the cameras, the coloured clothes, and, of course, the sunglasses. Jones was the first cricketer to wear sunglasses on the field, something that was frowned upon at the time. Everyone laughed at him. Now today on a bright, sunny day it's rare to see any cricketer without sunglasses on. He was a rebel who was prepared to take on tradition as well as the fastest bowlers and the best spinners.

Jones scored 145 at the Gabba against England in 1990. That high a score was unheard of at that time. A trademark move of Dean's was to advance down the pitch towards the ball as the fast bowler was running towards him. It was a real sign of intent and aggression against a bowler. It almost looked like he was dancing or skipping down the pitch, and then he would hit sixes and almost take one hand off the bat. They were standout innings, and I remember thinking it looked like he was having so much fun. Dean was a player who had a great time and took risks, and that's exactly what cricket is all about for me.

Many people try to rein in risk-takers in cricket. A common conversation around this is when people tell you to keep positive and back yourself, but to tone it down. That means they want you to stop taking risks. But I believe that with risks can come rewards and it's just a matter of learning when to take risks and when to play it safe. There is a time and a place for both. Dean Jones was a great risk-taker but he wasn't reckless. He took what we call 'calculated risk', where he knew he had the skills to back up the risk. There were times when he went in and would try to charge the first ball and whack the bowler. His Test match career shows that you can balance risk and reward – he played 52 Test matches with an average in the 40s and scored Test match centuries and double centuries.

I remember watching Dean play when I was a kid and thinking he was everything that was good about the game. Jones was a natural entertainer and I think he was as much an entertainer as he was a cricketer. A sport like cricket might seem to be about skill and technique, and there is no doubt how important they are. But it's also about fun and loving every minute you get to be out on that pitch. Dean Jones taught me that.

PLAYING CAREER

CAREER: 1984–1992 Test, 1984–1994 ODI
MATCHES: 52 Test, 164 ODI
RUNS: 3,631 Test runs, 6,068 ODI runs
CENTURIES & FIFTIES: 11 & 14 Test, 7 & 46 ODI
BATTING AVERAGE: 46.55 Test, 44.61 ODI
HIGH SCORE: 216 Test, 145 ODI
FIELDING: 34 Test dismissals (34 Ct), 54 ODI dismissals (54 Ct)

MEG LANNING

I look at the way Meg Lanning plays, and even walks and talks, and I think of Steve Waugh. Her batting strokes bring Steve to mind every time I watch her play. It's a compliment of the highest order.

**BORN 25 MARCH 1992
SINGAPORE**

MEG LANNING

RIGHT-HANDED TOP ORDER BATTER

Meg Lanning is a cricket superstar. From a young age, she has made a huge impact at both domestic and international levels.

Meg has a particularly strong slog sweep stroke that is just like Steve Waugh's. It's a stroke where you get down on one knee and hit the leg side. Your aim is to hit a four or a six and get it over the infield. The slog sweep became a trademark of Steve's and now Meg has taken it over. Meg plays that stroke with great strength and authority. From the moment Meg is up to bat she just gets out there really quickly, which I love to see. Meg has so much presence when she is at the crease. She just seems to want to get into the contest and try to start to dominate the opposition. I love her confident 'bring it on' mindset. And more often than not, she gets onto the pitch and dominates.

Sadly in women's cricket, players are starved of Test match opportunities. So we've only seen Meg play in four Test matches after making her Test debut in 2013. Meg is incredibly valuable in white-ball cricket and has the ability to take her time and defend and then flick the switch to a power game. She is remarkably consistent and produces impactful results in whatever format she plays.

One of my favourite Lanning moments is not one of her highest profile ones. She was the number one batter in the world and had been lured to the west by the Perth Scorchers as their prize recruit. There was one game at the WACA where the Scorchers were chasing a title – the run rate had built up and the pressure was building on Meg to get the job done. With all the pressure and expectation on her in that moment, she didn't look visibly phased at all. Then she resorted to that famous slog sweep and closed it out by hitting a six to win the game. I was so impressed by her trust in her skills to not be overwhelmed by all that pressure and to execute perfectly when her team needed it most. It might not be the highlight of her career but it says a lot about her.

In 2021, Lanning led the Australian women's team to set a new world record for the most consecutive One Day International victories. Until then, the record had been held by the team captained by Ricky Ponting that I played in, but I could not have been happier to see that record broken by Lanning's team. She is an inspiring leader and clearly knows how to get the most out of her team. She also leads by example and plays the game in a way that lifts those around her. As a player and captain, Lanning has carved out an extraordinary career.

PLAYING CAREER

*as of 18 July, 2021

CAREER: 2013–present Test, 2011–present ODI, 2010–present T20I

MATCHES: 4 Test, 85 ODI, 110 T20I

RUNS: 185 Test runs, 3,925 ODI runs, 2,914 T20I runs

CENTURIES & FIFTIES: 0 & 1 Test, 14 & 15 ODI, 2 & 13 T20I

BATTING AVERAGE: 23.12 Test, 53.76 ODI, 35.97 T20I

HIGH SCORE: 57 Test, 152* ODI, 133* T20I

FIELDING: 2 Test dismissals (2 Ct), 43 ODI dismissals (44 Ct), 39 T20I dismissals (39 Ct)

USMAN KHAWAJA

Usman is one of the most naturally gifted cricketers and batters to ever come through. The way he plays cricket is a pure joy to watch.

**BORN 18 DECEMBER 1986
ISLAMABAD, PAKISTAN**

USMAN KHAWAJA

LEFT-HANDED TOP ORDER BATTER

Much like his batting style, Usman Khawaja likes things to flow naturally. In the 2011 Ashes Test in Sydney, Khawaja became the first person of Pakistan origin to represent Australia. He also became the first Muslim to play for Australia. Being the first to do something can be lonely and hard. But there's no way around it – there needs to be a first so there can be a second and a third and a one-hundredth. As the game of cricket seeks to become more diverse and inclusive, players like Khawaja are leading the way. He may have been the first but he will not be the last.

Khawaja is a fluid and naturally gifted batter. Every stroke in his arsenal is a joy to watch almost every time he executes it. Sometimes it's hard to tell where Usman ends and the bat begins. I could watch him bat all day long.

The standout innings in Khawaja's career was in 2018 in a Test match against Pakistan played in the United Arab Emirates. Spoiler alert: he scored 100. But what was so remarkable about it (apart from the fact it's really hard to score 100 in a Test match) is that he did it in an innings that went a long way in preventing a loss for Australia and saving a match that seemed, until then, to not be savable. It was an absolute batting masterclass. Australia was down and out and just had to bat to survive. Tradition would say that is the time to play perfect textbook cricket and not to take any risks. Khawaja broke nearly every rule though, and it paid off. He came to the crease and started playing reverse sweeps, a stroke not widely used in Test cricket and much more typical in 20 over cricket. He did this because he thought it best to be aggressive and attack. Nobody expected him to bat like that in that situation. He used tactics, skill and aggression to turn around a match that seemed all but lost. Usman feels that the reverse sweep is as natural a stroke for him to play as the traditional front foot defensive stroke. He's right. The risk paid off. I firmly believe that had this innings taken place on Australian soil in front of a local crowd and been shown on Australian TV, people would talk about it with reverence and it would be thought of as being one of the top 20 Test match innings ever. That's certainly how I think of it.

Khawaja is very proud of his Pakistan heritage and Muslim faith. He now plays an active role as a multicultural leader in cricket. He is working hard to try to make the sport more diverse and inclusive. Khawaja is a great representative on and off the field and it's wonderful to have voices like his being heard as the sport changes to reflect diversity in Australia.

PLAYING CAREER

CAREER: 2011–2019 Test, 2013–2019 ODI, 2016–2016 T20I
MATCHES: 44 Test, 40 ODI, 9 T20I
RUNS: 2,887 Test runs, 1,554 ODI runs, 241 T20I runs
CENTURIES & FIFTIES: 8 & 14 Test, 2 & 12 ODI, 0 & 1 T20I
BATTING AVERAGE: 40.66 Test, 42.00 ODI, 26.77 T20I
HIGH SCORE: 174 Test, 104 ODI, 58 T20I
FIELDING: 35 Test dismissals (35 Ct), 13 ODI dismissals (13 Ct), 5 T20I dismissals (5 Ct)

ALLAN BORDER

A real hero of mine and a fellow left-handed batter. He is one of the greatest greats of the sport.

**BORN 27 JULY 1955
SYDNEY, NEW SOUTH WALES**

ALLAN BORDER

LEFT-HANDED MIDDLE ORDER BATTER

My first memory of Allan Border was when he forged a long and terrific last wicket partnership with Jeff Thomson in the 1981–82 Ashes in Melbourne against England. You would think that the memory I mention here would be of one of Border's many dominating moments. But actually, this time he and Thomson fell agonisingly short. Though they almost got Australia over the line, they just couldn't quite do it, and England won by three runs. Even so, I fell in love with Border in that match. His grit and determination left a lasting impression on me. And the showmanship and risk-taking from Border and Thomson completely caught my attention. How I would later play the game came from watching that last wicket moment when I was 11 years old.

A few years later in England in 1989, Border led the Ashes team to win. It was one of the great victories because Australia had been on the backfoot for so long. That team was described as one of the worst teams to arrive on English soil. They had won the 1987 World Cup, which was a bit of a surprise, but nobody thought they could win the 1989 Ashes. Seeing Allan Border being presented with that tiny Ashes urn was a symbolic moment.

I won the Allan Border medal in 2003. To win that medal meant the world to me because Border inspired me so much. I fell in love with the baggy green cap and the concept of possibly, just maybe, if I was good enough, playing for the Australian cricket team because of Allan Border. He made it look like hard work but good fun. He seemed like he enjoyed being in a team, and I think I learned the concept of team from him. Border is now a friend and colleague of mine. He is one of the nicest, gentlest, friendliest people you could meet.

Border remained consistent and loyal to the Australian cricket team throughout his career, even in very tough times. He trained as hard as he could and he played as hard as he could. He was a reluctant captain and an accidental hero. He was known as Captain Grumpy during his captaincy days and although that might have been what was needed in that time, he has mellowed. He commanded great respect, and through hard work and determination he got Australian cricket out of some troubled times. He is the godfather of Australian cricket.

PLAYING CAREER

CAREER: 1978–1994 Test, 1979–1994 ODI
MATCHES: 156 Tests, 273 ODIs
RUNS: 11,174 Test runs, 6,524 ODI runs
CENTURIES & FIFTIES: 27 & 63 Test, 3 & 39 ODI
BATTING AVERAGE: 50.56 Test, 30.62 ODI
HIGH SCORE: 205 Test, 127* ODI
FIELDING: 156 Test dismissals (156 Ct), 127 ODI dismissals (127 Ct)

STEVE SMITH

It's not every day you get to witness the transformation of someone from a leg-spin bowler to one of the best batters of modern cricket.

**BORN 2 JUNE 1989
ST GEORGE, NEW SOUTH WALES**

STEVE SMITH

RIGHT-HANDED MIDDLE ORDER BATTER

Steve Smith started his cricketing career as a blond-haired, portly leg-spin bowler. Does that sound like anyone else mentioned in this book? If your answer is Glenn McGrath then you're very wrong, but if your answer is Shane Warne then you couldn't be more correct. Steve Smith did look to be an ideal replacement for Shane Warne. But not everything works out how you think it might.

Smith seemed to know deep down that he had a batter within him despite everyone paying attention to his bowling. He progressed from number eight to be in the top six batsmen. But then, as with many great cricketers early in their careers, he was dropped. Smith went away to work on and develop his technique. But instead of perfecting textbook-perfect technique, he decided to build his own style in his own way. Once he worked out his style, he had complete belief in it and his technique. The results he has achieved speak for themselves – he is currently statistically matching Donald Bradman.

So let's take a closer look at Smith's technique. It may look awkward and fidgety – he has his own mannerisms that are the opposite to what you're told about movement and body positioning in traditional cricket. But when you look closer you realise that at the crucial moment when the bat meets the ball, Smith's body and head end up exactly where you want them to be in the textbook version of the stroke. There's a lot of moving around to get to that position but Smith is nearly always exactly where he needs to be when he's actually hitting the ball. And at the end of the day, that's all that matters.

Steve made some poor decisions in South Africa in 2018. He took responsibility for what became known as the 'sandpaper scandal' and was banned from playing for 12 months and from a leadership position for two years. In the year he was banned from playing, he spent a lot of time speaking in schools and working with charities. When Smith returned to play cricket, he was not only under the microscope of the cricketing community – people all over the world, even outside of cricket, had heard what had happened. The focus on Steve could not have been stronger. But his was one of the most extraordinary comebacks I have ever seen. Smith's first Test after his 12-month ban was played in the Ashes series in England in 2019. Smith scored 100 in each innings. He did that with the entire world watching him, and the 40,000-odd English supporters in the crowd booing him, reminding him of the mistake he had made. His mental strength to push everything that had happened aside and to just focus on every delivery was nothing short of extraordinary. His batting in both innings was exemplary. We all make mistakes but it's how we handle ourselves in the aftermath that reveal who we are.

PLAYING CAREER

*as of 18 July, 2021

CAREER: 2010–present Test, ODI & T20I
MATCHES: 77 Test, 128 ODI, 45 T20I
RUNS: 7,540 Test runs, 4,378 ODI runs, 794 T20I runs
CENTURIES & FIFTIES: 27 & 31 Test, 11 & 25 ODI, 0 & 4 T20I runs
BATTING AVERAGE: 61.80 Test, 43.34 ODI, 27.37 T20I
HIGH SCORE: 239 Test, 164 ODI, 90 T20I
FIELDING: 12 Test dismissals (123 Ct), 70 ODI dismissals (70 Ct), 29 T20I dismissals (29 Ct),

CHRIS LYNN

GILLY SAYS

Chris was one of the first guys to target being a Twenty20 specialist. So powerful and skilful is his game that he sparked interest around the world in this new format of cricket.

BORN 10 APRIL 1990
BRISBANE, QUEENSLAND

CHRIS LYNN

RIGHT-HANDED BATTER

Chris Lynn is a true modern-day cricketer. He has had a successful first-class cricket career, but he was also one of the first players to target becoming a Twenty20 specialist. Lynn is such an excitement-machine of a player. It's impossible not to watch him play, and you never want to miss a ball. His approach has always been attack, attack, attack. It's a high risk approach and coaches and others may want to rein it in. But Lynn always stays true to who he is and how he wants to play. It's great entertainment and I love to watch Lynn do his thing.

The Twenty20 revolution may well change cricket forever, and Lynn has been a pioneer of this new format of the game. Cricket has changed over the years. Test cricket was formed well over 100 years ago and is played over five consecutive days. One-day cricket started in the 1970s and now includes Twenty20 cricket, which is played over three hours. Twenty20 cricket is an exciting new development. It showcases players' power and skills in a different way and it makes sense for some players to be better suited to it than others. There is room to have expertise in different formats. A player like Lynn who can perform well in all formats of the game may well be considered among the greatest players of all time.

Whenever I think of Lynn, I picture him playing in the Big Bash for Brisbane Heat at the Gabba (Brisbane Cricket Ground). He hit a ball off Shaun Tait and it sailed clean over the roof! It was mesmerising. If you view the footage of this moment, you'll watch as the camera searches for the ball, which had cleared the roof, and then goes back to Lynn and zooms in on his face. He looks a little expressionless, glances over at Tait, and then gives a little wink. It was such an iconic moment: that huge hit and then just a little wink. Lynn is a very laidback guy who was enjoying himself in the moment, which made it a spectacular thing to watch.

It says a lot about Lynn's character that he saw Twenty20 cricket as where his skills might be best utilised. Lynn's shoulder injury issues made it hard for him to launch a Test cricket career – being fit and at the top of your game for five-day Test cricket is not easy. His dream might have been to play Test cricket for Australia but the way he pursued Twenty20 cricket shows you that dreams can change, and you need to make the most of the opportunities that come your way. Lynn is now one of the best and most exciting Twenty20 players to watch.

PLAYING CAREER

as of 18 July, 2021

CAREER: 2014–present T20I
MATCHES: 18 T20Is, 41 First Class
RUNS: 291 T20I runs, 2,743 First Class runs
CENTURIES & FIFTIES: 6 & 12 First Class
BATTING AVERAGE: 19.39 T20I, 43.53 First Class
HIGH SCORE: 44 T20I, 250 First Class
FIELDING: 3 ODI dismissals (3 Ct), 3 T20I dismissals (3 Ct)

GLENN MAXWELL

What a talent. You just never know what is going to happen when he walks to the crease. He's an excitement machine.

**BORN 14 OCTOBER 1988
MELBOURNE, VICTORIA**

GLENN MAXWELL

RIGHT-HANDED BATTING ALLROUNDER

When Glenn Maxwell walks to the crease, there is so much anticipation around what might happen. It could be one of the most majestic, entertaining evenings. He could completely invent a new shot. Maxwell's skill level is so high, but where he really thrives is in his creativity. Here is a player who has taken the old cricket textbook and said, 'Thanks for the foundation but now I'm going to write a completely new book of what's possible'. It's inspirational for former players like myself and for every newcomer to the game. This guy is a true pioneer. He is playing with complete freedom and even the most reluctant traditionalist has to take notice of what he's doing and be amazed by what he's capable of.

There was a lot of pressure on Maxwell from a young age. He was a talented player and everyone saw his potential. With big expectations comes a lot of pressure, and it's a burden that Maxwell carried. He may have been moving up through the cricketing ranks, but that doesn't mean it has been a smooth journey.

It was hard for Maxwell to deal with speed bumps like a run of bad results or being dropped from a team. I think he knew that the pressure to perform was clouding his mind so much that it was affecting his cricket, his attitude, his mental health and his life away from the game. I think he was so courageous to identify that and then to speak openly about it. Maxwell took some time away from the game to clear his head before he came back. A number of cricketers and other sportspeople have been able to do that in recent years, which has inspired others to assess their own mental health and how they're going.

Now Maxwell's back and seems to be playing with a great deal more fun. In the last few years since he identified his mental health struggles, he's come back into leadership positions and as captain. He is doing an outstanding job. It's a credit to him that when he knew he was ready to come back, he did so and in a big way. He wanted to play a big part and it's great to watch him relishing the responsibility as a captain. And we get to sit back and be so entertained and inspired by how he plays the game – his way.

Every innings that Maxwell bats is extraordinary. We have him to thank for so many of the innovative shots in modern-day cricket, and the game of cricket is better for having players like him.

PLAYING CAREER
*as of 18 July, 2021

CAREER: 2013–present Test, 2012–present ODI & T20I
MATCHES: 7 Tests, 116 ODIs, 72 T20Is
RUNS: 339 Test runs, 3,320 ODI runs, 1,780 T20I runs
BATTING AVERAGE: 26.07 Test, 34.36 ODI, 31.78 T20I
HIGH SCORE: 104 Test, 108 ODI, 145* T20I
WICKETS: 8 Test wickets, 51 ODI wickets, 31 T20I wickets
BEST HAUL: 4/127 Test, 4/46 ODI, 3/10 T20I
BOWLING AVERAGE: 42.62 Test, 52.60 ODI, 26.16 T20I
FIELDING: 5 Test dismissals (5 Ct), 72 ODI dismissals (72 Ct), 35 T20I dismissals (35 Ct)

MARNUS LABUSCHAGNE

The man who never stops talking and thinking about cricket. He's mad for it!

**BORN 22 JUNE 1994
KLERKSDORP, NORTH WEST PROVINCE,
SOUTH AFRICA**

46

MARNUS LABUSCHAGNE

RIGHT-HANDED BATTING ALLROUNDER

Marnus Labuschagne was born in South Africa and came to Australia with his family when he was 10 years old. That's usually a couple of years before the time people who go on to become professional cricketers start to take the sport seriously. He was a talented young player but he didn't stand out from his peers at that time. Still, he worked his way through the ranks and played some State cricket. When Marnus got picked for Australia in 2018, it was a bit of a shock as he had not really shown his strengths yet. It was at a time when Steve Smith and David Warner were out of the team due to suspensions. With that came opportunity for other players, and Marnus was ready to jump in and make the most of that opportunity.

Labuschagne might only be five years younger than Steve Smith but he has tried to learn from and mirror Smith as much as possible. He has put so much effort into that and it has got him some great results. Marnus's batting technique may not be textbook perfect, and he has similar mannerisms to Steve Smith, but his game is rooted in strong defensive play. It is a patience game for Marnus. He just wants to get in there and bat and bat and bat and bat. He has the mental toughness to keep at it. I've noticed that he talks to himself when he's on the field. He might talk to teammates and opponents too, but he talks to himself to motivate himself and keep focused. He's a busy player – always paying attention to what's happening and thinking about what might happen next. He gives his all in everything he does and you know he's always working at 100 per cent.

A really significant moment in Marnus's career came when Steve Smith was back in the team and Marnus was first reserve. It was the second Ashes Test match at Lord's in 2019. Smith got hit in the helmet with the ball and had to retire hurt. Marnus came in as a concussion replacement to bat when Steve Smith was ruled out for the rest of the game. Marnus also took a blow to the helmet, but he was okay to keep playing. He went on to dominate that series and ever since then he has gone on to dominate Test cricket. It was a landmark moment for him. Stepping in like that against an English bowling line-up, with players such as Jofra Archer – who was bowling extremely quick and really aggressively – was no easy task. And the best thing was, you could see how much Marnus was loving it. He might have taken a blow to the head himself but you wouldn't have known it from how he was playing.

Marnus lives and breathes cricket. He still plays a lot of backyard cricket with his friends (and sometimes his dog!) to keep the fun in the game. He shows that if you work hard and you enjoy what you do, you can keep improving your skills to become the best you can be.

PLAYING CAREER

*as of 18 July, 2021

CAREER: 2018–present Test, 2020–present ODI
MATCHES: 18 Tests, 13 ODIs, 94 FC
RUNS: 1,885 Test runs, 473 ODI runs, 6,999 FC runs
CENTURIES & FIFTIES: 5 & 10 Test, 1 & 3 ODI, 18 & 38 FC
BATTING AVERAGE: 60.80 Test, 39.41 ODI, 45.74 FC
HIGH SCORE: 215 Test, 108 DI, 215 FC
BEST HAUL: 3/45 Test, 3/45 FC
BOWLING AVERAGE: 41.66 Test, 44.93 FC
WICKETS: 12 Test wickets, 62 FC wickets
FIELDING: 15 Test dismissals (15 Ct), 4 ODI dismissals (4 Ct), 84 FC dismissals (84 Ct)

BETH MOONEY

A truly versatile allrounder who consistently performs at the highest level. Beth's an exciting risk taker who has the skills to back it up. She is the ultimate competitor.

**BORN 14 JANUARY 1994
SHEPPARTON, VICTORIA**

BETH MOONEY

WICKETKEEPER & LEFT-HANDED BATTER

Beth Mooney is one of the great crop of current women cricketers who have come in and raised the skill level and entertainment value of the game. In Twenty20 cricket, Mooney opens the batting and is at the top of the order. And for good reason. She's also a wicketkeeper and a strong batter in 50-over cricket. She's a consistent performer and a versatile cricketer, and she's of huge value to any team. It makes sense that she won Player of the Tournament at the women's Twenty20 World Cup in 2020.

Mooney is a highly skilled batter. She has a lot of versatility in her stroke play. Mooney uses her feet really well and hits the ball in the air over fielders. She is able to manipulate the ball around the field in a very proactive manner. A feature of her game is that her mind is always busy looking for ways to get the scoreboard moving. She often seems able to find gaps to hit to. She's also a risk-taker and is happy to take risks for the team.

A standout performance in Beth's career was in the women's World Cup final at the Melbourne Cricket Ground in 2020. Beth walked onto the ground in front of 80,000 people and the global cricketing audience and she looked like she was born for that moment. Beth and her opening partner Alyssa Healy were so well prepared that they could just relax, enjoy it and let their skills shine through. Beth scored 78 not out at the top of the order, a record-breaking performance. Every moment of the final was a joy to watch. I had been in touch with Beth in the lead-up to the final and it was a true privilege to be on that journey with her and the team, if only in a small way.

Mooney really steps up in big games and is particularly good under pressure. In fact, she seems to thrive under pressure. It strikes me that she does a lot of reflection on her performances, and I think she spends a lot of time analysing both positive and negative results. This means that when she is faced with big moments like World Cup finals, she has analysed and assessed everything beforehand. She spends time mentally preparing so when the moment is before her, she can go out and enjoy it. There's also nothing like the last match in a tournament. It's the time to leave everything on the field and relax and let your skills shine through. That is exactly what Beth Mooney did and I have no doubt she'll be doing it many times over in her career.

PLAYING CAREER

*as of 18 July, 2021

CAREER: 2017-present Test, 2016-present ODI & T20I
MATCHES: 2 Test, 41 ODI, 58 T20I
RUNS: 1,170 ODI, 1,554 T20I
CENTURIES & FIFTIES: 1 & 8 ODI, 2 & 10 T20I
BATTING AVERAGE: 39.00 ODI, 36.13 T20I
HIGH SCORE: 100 ODI, 117* T20I
FIELDING: 14 ODI dismissals (14 Ct), 24 T20I dismissals (24 Ct)

TIM PAINE

I have so much respect for Tim Paine. He has been the exact kind of leader the team needed at a difficult time. He's also the player you want on your team when you're in a bit of trouble.

GILLY SAYS

**BORN 8 DECEMBER 1984
HOBART, TASMANIA**

TIM PAINE

RIGHT-HANDED WICKETKEEPER BATTER

Tim Paine's cricket journey has been defined by his mental and physical toughness to stick at it. He had a taste of playing for Australia early in his career before he suffered what seemed like a minor finger injury, though the injury was more serious than people realised and it looked like he would have to give up the game at one stage. But he stuck with it, worked hard and did everything possible to keep playing. Tim loves playing cricket and it was this love that motivated him to keep pushing on. He wanted to have the experience of playing for his country again, and that made him push himself and work his way back. His persistence is a credit to him.

What Tim did after coming in as captain following the unfortunate situation in South Africa in 2018 was nothing short of brilliant. He led the team both on and off the field, and he managed the public side of being captain. He is a very disciplined leader, which is what the team needed when he was called on to become captain. It was a tough position to come into at a very difficult time and he should be commended for the wonderful job he did under a lot of pressure.

Tim's consistency is something I greatly admire. He's a beautiful cricketer to watch. He has all the textbook-perfect batting strokes and can play them as well as anyone. His wicketkeeping is of an exceptionally high standard. He's so often playing his role exactly right that it's easy for him to go unnoticed, but I always see his consistency. His stats speak for themselves, especially with the gloves. I love seeing a wicketkeeper at the top of their game, giving it their all. His contribution just lifts everyone.

One of the things I admire most about Paine is how thoughtful he is when he speaks. He wants to be open and to give meaningful answers to questions. He is also very quick to speak about and try to fix mistakes. He wants to learn from them, improve on them and move on. Mistakes are a part of life, and a part of sport, and how we handle mistakes is the most important thing. Tim's handling of mistakes and his persistence through difficult times is a fine example of his leadership as a cricketer and as a person.

PLAYING CAREER

*as of 18 July, 2021

CAREER: 2010–present Test, 2009–2018 ODI, 2009–2017 T20I
MATCHES: 35 Tests, 35 ODIs, 12 T20Is
RUNS: 1,534 Test Runs, 890 ODI Runs
BATTING AVERAGE: 32.63 Test, 27.81 ODI, 10.25 T20I
HIGH SCORE: 92 Test, 111 ODI, 25 T20I
CENTURIES & FIFTIES: 0 & 9 Test, 1 & 5 ODI
KEEPING: 157 Test dismissals (150 Ct, 7 St), 55 ODI Dismissals (51 Ct, 4 St), 13 T20I Dismissals (11 Ct, 2 St)

ALYSSA HEALY

Such an inspiring story that has helped bring a new level of exposure to the game.

**BORN 24 MARCH 1990
GOLD COAST, QUEENSLAND**

ALYSSA HEALY

RIGHT-HANDED WICKETKEEPER BATTER

Alyssa Healy has cricket in her DNA. Her dad was a cricketer and her uncle, Ian Healy, was Australia's Test wicketkeeper. It's extraordinary how similar her mannerisms are to Ian's. When I watch the way she wicketkeeps, walks, moves and takes a throw from the outfield, it feels like I'm watching Ian. It's no wonder she's the best in the world at what she does.

Alyssa built on the foundations of the cricket 'textbook' but brought in modern day risk-taking and a carefree batting approach, which has been absolutely brilliant. She brought a very exciting skill set to the women's game: she made it all about power and risk. By doing so, she took the game to the next level and led the action-packed games we see today. Alyssa worked on developing really powerful strokes. To see women's players like Healy scoring at a rate we've become accustomed to in men's cricket made a lot of people pay attention. And her risk-taking is so fun to watch. With great risk can come great rewards – something I always believed in my playing days. Alyssa reminds us these are the reasons we play cricket, and you should just go out there and back yourself, no matter who you are.

Alyssa is wonderful batting, but she's something special over the stumps. A lot of the wicketkeeping we see in the women's game is over the stumps (though that is changing as faster bowlers are coming in). At the stumps, wicketkeeping is all about body positioning, glove work and head position. It takes a lot of practice and a lot of work on technique and refining and honing skill. Wicketkeepers need to concentrate fully at all times. It has been exceptional to see Alyssa keeping the standard that she has set and maintained. She is an expert wicketkeeper over the stumps. Alyssa likes to be involved in every ball, which is exactly what's needed for a wicketkeeper. She has a true fighting spirit, which is also needed; she loves a good contest and taking on a challenge. Like me, she may have wanted to be a fast bowler when she was younger but finding a strong position for yourself behind the stumps makes for exciting cricket.

Healy is a born cricketer. And to be so good at wicket and with a bat makes her a versatile and exciting player. Her records speak for themselves, but what Alyssa shows is that a love of the sport, a willingness to take risks and a drive to refine skill and technique can all have huge results. She's always quick to credit her bowler teammates with any of her successes or records, but she deserves all the credit that comes her way.

PLAYING CAREER

*as of 18 July, 2021

• • •

CAREER: 2011–present Test, 2010–present ODI & T20I
MATCHES: 4 Tests, 79 ODIs, 118 T20Is
RUNS: 201 Test Runs, 1,927 ODI Runs, 2,121 T20I runs
BATTING AVERAGE: 33.50 Test, 33.80 ODI, 24.66 T20I
HIGH SCORE: 58 Test, 133 ODI, 148* T20I
CENTURIES & FIFTIES: 0 & 1 Test, 3 & 12 ODI, 1 & 12 T20I
KEEPING: 8 Test dismissals (7 Ct, 1 St), 78 ODI Dismissals (54 Ct, 24 St), 97 T20I Dismissals (46 Ct, 51 St)

PAT CUMMINS

What a package he has turned out to be! Such persistence and determination in a player who burst onto the scene in the most exciting way possible.

GILLY SAYS

BORN 8 MAY 1993
SYDNEY, NEW SOUTH WALES

PAT CUMMINS

RIGHT-ARM FAST BOWLER

If you are passionate, determined, committed and prepared to do the hard work, you can achieve anything. Pat Cummins shows us all how true this is. He is such a wonderful example of how to work through setbacks and disappointments, and I'm constantly inspired by him.

Pat burst onto the scene as an 18-year-old when he debuted for Australia in South Africa. He picked up a six wicket haul on his debut, seven wickets in the match. He was out on the crease when Australia hit the winning runs. It was a dream debut. But then he suffered stress fractures that ruled him out for a long time. It was about five years before he was back in the Australian team, and even once he was back he could only play a limited amount of cricket. But he continued to work on his technique and to learn as much as he could about injury prevention and rehabilitation. He worked on his fitness and strengthened his body. There must have been moments during those five years when he wondered if he would ever play for Australia again. It shows how strong he is mentally and physically that he was able to make such an impressive comeback and never give up.

When you come into a sport at a young age, you will find people have lots of opinions about the way you play, whether you're doing well or doing badly. We all need to remember that young players are still learning.

Pat is a great example of a young player who has continued to learn and improve. I am impressed by Pat's reliability and consistency. When pressure needs to be applied, Pat is your man – he reminds me a bit of

Glenn McGrath in that way! He will consistently and repeatedly apply pressure to batters with disciplined tight bowling. It doesn't matter if you're behind or ahead in the game, you can rely on Cummins.

Pat is just a class act in everything he does. He's among the best fast bowlers in the world, and he has developed into a fine allrounder with his batting and fielding skills and his athleticism generally. He is able to play both white-ball and red-ball formats and to be one of the best players on the field. Everybody respects Pat and sees how hard he works. He plays an active role in the leadership group and he leads by example. And what an example he sets!

PLAYING CAREER

*as of 18 July, 2021

CAREER: 2011–present Test, ODI & T20I
MATCHES: 34 Tests, 69 ODIs, 30 T20Is
WICKETS: 164 Test Wickets, 111 ODI Wickets, 37 T20I Wickets
WICKETS IN AN INNINGS & MATCH: 5 five w/inns, 1 ten w/match Test, 1 five w/inns ODI
BOWLING AVERAGE: 21.59 Test, 28.78 ODI, 20.62 T20I
BEST HAUL: 6/23 Test, 5/70 ODI, 3/15 T20I
BATTING: 708 Test runs, 285 ODI runs, 48 T20I runs
BATTING AVERAGE: 16.46 Test, 9.82 ODI
FIELDING: 16 Test dismissals (16 Ct), 16 ODI dismissals (16Ct), 9 T20I dismissals (9 Ct)

DENNIS LILLEE

Seeing Dennis come steaming in, shirt unbuttoned, gold chain flying, sweat dripping down the side of the brow and his hair flying in the wind was one of the great sights of cricket.

**BORN 18 JULY 1949
SUBIACO, WESTERN AUSTRALIA**

DENNIS LILLEE

RIGHT-ARM FAST BOWLER

After watching Dennis Lillee bowl, I decided as a young boy that I was going to be the fastest bowler in history. It didn't quite turn out that way, but he was an original inspiration for my cricketing dreams. After seeing a pair of wicketkeeping gloves in a sports store in Shepparton, I decided the other part of the bowling partnership was for me – wicketkeeping. Which is a good thing because I wasn't very good at fast bowling! You know who was a great fast bowler though? Dennis Lillee. He was aggressive, athletic and so entertaining.

Dennis was Australian cricket to me. I grew up thinking he was the greatest fast bowler in the world. And at the peak of his career, he was. By the time Lillee retired, he held the world record 355 Test wickets.

He's always been direct in his opinion and stuck to what he thinks is right and how he wants to play. I've always admired him for this.

Lillee played at a time of change in cricket, and he influenced some of this change. World Series Cricket was being established and encouraging more public interest in the sport, and Lillee was a part of this new format of the game. During this time, he was a key person in making cricket a professional sport, meaning players would be paid for playing, and would earn enough to make a living. Lillee fought for players' rights and his work in this area has made professional cricket what it is today. Every professional player owes Lillee gratitude for their careers.

Lillee was the greatest appealer in the game. At the Melbourne Boxing Day Test in 1981, he bowled the last ball to Vivian Richards and bowled him out. Lillee kept running and sprinting, and his teammates charged in to join him. It was such a great moment. And that, combined with his strong appeal to the umpire, would have made him very hard to say no to.

As well as inspiring me, Lillee certainly inspired other people to the game. He had a huge impact through his playing career, and he has made a significant contribution to cricket on a global scale, including helping to set up a fast bowling academy in India. He was always prepared to share his knowledge and experience, and we're seeing the incredible results of his work today.

I am lucky enough now to call Dennis a friend. I still get a little thrill when Dennis Lillee calls me! Sometimes in life, your heroes become your friends. Little me in the backyard dreaming of bowling like Dennis Lillee had no idea what the future held. Who knows what might be in store for you?

PLAYING CAREER

CAREER: 1971–1984 Test, 1972–1983 ODI

MATCHES: 70 Tests, 63 ODIs

WICKETS: 355 Test wickets, 103 ODI wickets

WICKETS IN AN INNINGS & MATCH: 23 five w/inns & 7 10 w/match Test, 1 five w/inns ODI

BOWLING AVERAGE: 23.92 Test, 20.82 ODI

BEST HAUL: 7/83 Test, 5/34 ODI

BATTING: 905 Test runs, 240 ODI runs

BATTING AVERAGE: 13.71 Test, 9.23 ODI

FIELDING: 23 Test dismissals (23 Ct), 10 ODI dismissals (10 Ct)

JOSH HAZLEWOOD

Being compared to Glenn McGrath is one of the highest accolades. I love Josh's calmness and his control. He is the ultimate team player.

GILLY SAYS

**BORN 8 JANUARY 1991
TAMWORTH, NEW SOUTH WALES**

JOSH HAZLEWOOD

RIGHT-ARM FAST MEDIUM BOWLER

Josh Hazlewood became the youngest ever fast bowler to represent New South Wales in 2008, aged just 17. Since then, Hazlewood has often been compared to Glenn McGrath. Both come from small country towns and the way they bowl is very similar. It's a great compliment to be compared to someone like Glenn McGrath, and nobody makes that comparison lightly. It's no wonder that McGrath is Josh's idol.

Like McGrath, Hazlewood is an incredibly consistent and reliable bowler. The greatest thing we look for in cricket is consistency and accuracy. You need to be able to execute your skill as close to perfect as many times as possible. Perfection might seem like an impossible goal but it's what every cricketer is working at. What Hazlewood has perfected is his ability to apply pressure to an opponent. And that gets results, either for him or for one of his teammates. You might not be able to see pressure reflected in the stats, but when you are in a team you can recognise the players that can execute their skills in a way that builds so much pressure on their opponents. It changes the game, and Hazlewood is that kind of bowler. He's calm and consistent and his whole team can rely on him.

Hazlewood is the ultimate teammate and he clearly loves being part of a team. He's not looking to steal the limelight or draw attention to himself. He is happy to do the work needed to play at his best, and he is willing to do that hard work day in and day out and then enjoy the success of the team. The current era of players like Mitchell Starc, Pat Cummins, Nathan Lyon and Josh Hazlewood are a close-knit group and they clearly love playing together. As I reflect on my career, I realise how lucky I was to experience that same joy with my teammates on the national team. Cricket is probably the most individual sport in a team game. At the end of the day, bowlers are bowling by themselves and batters are batting by themselves. But it's also a game of partnerships. And bowlers like Hazlewood who are such good team players are leading the way.

When Hazlewood is not playing cricket, he's a great darts player! His accuracy makes him very good at throwing darts as well as cricket balls. I'm a huge admirer of this young bowler. It's great to see someone who loves the sport and the spirit of the game and who plays so consistently well. That's my favourite kind of player.

PLAYING CAREER
*as of 18 July, 2021

CAREER: 2014–present Test, 2010–present ODI, 2013–present T20
MATCHES: 55 Tests, 54 ODIs, 13 T20Is
WICKETS: 212 Test wickets, 88 ODI wickets, 13 T20I
WICKETS IN AN INNINGS & MATCH: 9 five w/inns Test, 3 five w/inns ODI
BOWLING AVERAGE: 25.65 Test, 26.18 ODI, 34.38 T20I
BEST HAUL: 6/67 Test, 6/52 ODI, 4/30 T20I
BATTING: 445 Test runs, 53 ODI runs
BATTING AVERAGE: 12.02 Test, 17.66 ODI
FIELDING: 19 Test dismissals (19 Ct), 16 ODI dismissals (16 Ct)

GLENN McGRATH

Merv Hughes was the biggest pest of his era. Glenn McGrath happily took over that mantle. He was so mischievous and always a jokester. Oh, and he's definitely the person you want on your team.

GILLY SAYS

**BORN 9 FEBRUARY 1970
DUBBO, NSW**

GLENN McGRATH

RIGHT-ARM FAST MEDIUM BOWLER

The highlight of my career may have been being a wicketkeeper to Shane Warne, but doing the same with Glenn McGrath is a very, very, very close second. One of the great sights in cricket is a fast bowler steaming in after a long run-up and all that build-up, and then their explosion of pace and energy. As a wicketkeeper, it's a totally different skill set keeping for a fast bowler compared with a spin bowler. With a fast bowler you're 20 metres back from the wicket. You might have more time to move but that ball is coming in fast. It's spectacular to be part of; so dramatic and so fun.

Conditions in Australia are particularly well suited to fast bowling. And even though Glenn may not have been the fastest bowler, he was so consistent and accurate. You knew you were in the game with every ball he bowled. He was a master at building pressure on a batter and consistently attacking to the point where the batter needed to try something different, and that was often risky. He just never let a batter relax. Not all bowlers can command that kind of attention.

McGrath's mischievous moments are well documented. Many times while I or another player was being interviewed in front of a TV camera, Glenn would be pelting us with grapes or cherries or anything he could get his hands on. It made concentrating for the interview very hard! He also loved to walk behind you and tap one of your shoulders, so you'd look over that shoulder only to find he was on your other side. They were classic little brother pranks and we loved him for it. As serious as professional sport can be, it's still important to be having fun with your friends.

An iconic moment for McGrath's bowling was at the WACA (Western Australian Cricket Association Ground) against the West Indies in the season of 2000–01. In the space of three deliveries he picked up his 300th wicket – the wicket of one of the top batters in the world, Brian Lara – and a hat-trick, all of which are hard to come by in Test cricket. It was a magical moment and the atmosphere was just electric. That little sequence of deliveries summed up McGrath's ruthlessness and the pressure that he put on opposing batters. He was so accurate from the very first delivery, and that mounted pressure and challenged the batters. He often got incredibly good results from that.

A major part of Glenn's life after cricket has been the McGrath Foundation. It's a wonderful legacy and testament to his wife Jane, who battled cancer. The support the Foundation receives from the government, the corporate world and the general public is inspirational. Glenn's hard work with the Foundation is a reflection of how he was as a cricketer and how he is as a person.

PLAYING CAREER

CAREER: 1993–2007 (Test and ODI)
MATCHES: 124 Tests, 250 ODIs
WICKETS: 563 Test wickets, 381 ODI wickets
WICKETS IN AN INNINGS & MATCH: 29 five w/inns & 3 ten w/match Test, 7 five w/inns ODI
BOWLING AVERAGE: 21.64 Test, 22.02 ODI
BEST HAUL: 8/24 Test, 7/15 ODI
BATTING: 641 Test runs, 115 ODI runs
BATTING AVERAGE: 7.36 Test, 3.83 ODI
FIELDING: 38 Test dismissals (38 Ct), 37 ODI dismissals (37 Ct)

SHANE WARNE

> The highlight of my cricketing career was being wicketkeeper to Shane Warne. Simple as that.

GILLY SAYS

BORN 13 SEPTEMBER 1969
MELBOURNE, VICTORIA

SHANE WARNE

RIGHT-ARM LEG SPIN BOWLER

I will never forget how it felt to crouch behind the wicket while Shane Warne bowled towards me. It was theatre. It was like watching a performer at their finest and I got to be in the front row. I loved seeing Warne right at the top of his bowling mark, with the nervous batter in my line of sight. The build-up to Warnie's delivery was magical. He always looked so confident and assured in what he was about to produce. It was all about the timing and the delivery, and he would vary it with each bowl. He did that so perfectly and it was mesmerising each time. It made my partnership with him so much fun.

I worked so hard to try to know what Shane was bowling, but there's a big difference between knowing what's coming and being in the right position to catch it. The more you wicketkeep to a particular bowler, the more you build up a familiarity with how they bowl. Shane had formed a record-breaking partnership with Ian Healy prior to me coming in. I was nervous about how to maintain that. I asked Warne to bowl more to me at training so I could become familiar with his style. And I was so grateful he did that. It allowed us to forge a very successful partnership, one that I think we're both very proud of.

Warne changed the cricketing landscape with his ball of the century, the 'Gatting ball'. He bowled to England's Mike Gatting in the 1993 series. The ball was a perfect example of the leg-spinner's art, pitching towards the far outside of the leg stump. But when the ball hit the turf it spun past the bat to hit Gatting's off-stump. That one ball stands out, but Warne bowled that exact delivery so many times throughout his career. He was such a consistent deliverer of balls just like that. He completely revived the art of spin bowling.

Warne might have only eaten pizza, hot chips and toasted sandwiches throughout his cricketing career, and maybe even still now, but he always knew what he liked and who he was and stuck to it. His mental toughness and determination added so much to the team. I remember an Ashes Test match in Adelaide in 2006–07, where after four days it looked like it was going to be a pretty boring draw. In our team warm-up, and in partnership with John Buchanan, Warne rallied us all to believe there was an opportunity for us to try to win the game that day. And then he came out and bowled this magical spell. We went on and late that day we won a remarkable Test that is now referred to as 'Amazing Adelaide'. And all because Warne was so headstrong and believed we could do it. This was a standout performance of his among so many.

We're seeing Warnie's legacy in the women's game. Young female cricketers taking up leg spin bowling is brilliant to see. Here's hoping the next Warnie is out there – I can't wait to meet her.

PLAYING CAREER

CAREER: 1992–2007 Test, 1993–2005 ODI
MATCHES: 145 Tests, 194 ODIs
WICKETS: 708 Test Wickets, 293 ODI Wickets
WICKETS IN AN INNINGS & MATCH: 37 five w/inns / 10 ten w/match Test, 1 five w/inns ODI
BOWLING AVERAGE: 25.41 Test, 25.73 ODI
BEST HAUL: 8/71 Test, 5/33 ODI
BATTING: 3154 Test runs, 1018 ODI runs
BATTING AVERAGE: 17.32 Test, 13.05 ODI
FIELDING: 125 Test dismissals (125 Ct), 80 ODI dismissals (80 Ct)

FAWAD AHMED

An absolutely outstanding leg spin bowler. A humble and generous person who overcame huge personal challenges.

**BORN 5 FEBRUARY 1982
SWABI, PAKISTAN**

FAWAD AHMED

RIGHT-ARM LEG SPIN BOWLER

Fawad Ahmed played some first class cricket in Pakistan before resettling in Melbourne. He fled Pakistan in 2010 after it became clear it was no longer safe for him to stay there. He arrived in Australia as an asylum seeker and in 2012 he was granted permanent residency. Fawad is a courageous person. He comes from a background that many of us growing up in Australia could never fathom: a war-torn country. He came to a completely new country in pursuit of a safe life and a dream. It's so wonderful that he was welcomed in Australia and he has made the most of every opportunity.

One of those opportunities was for Fawad to fill the void left by Shane Warne of quality leg spin bowling. Ahmed may not have had the variety of tricks Warnie did, but he executed the ones he did have with real consistency. He consistently bowled a good leg break, which meant pressure mounted on the batter. Ahmed does not have all the gusto and fanfare of Warnie's style – he's almost a silent operator – but he always bowls the best ball he has in his repertoire. The hardest art in cricket is bowling leg spin and he's incredibly skilled at that art.

Seeing Ahmed selected for Sheffield Shield cricket to play for Victoria was wonderful. He showed great strength of character, commitment and dedication. And I think he brings great balance and perspective to his game. He is always striving for the best result on the field, and he is able to quickly process what happens in a match. Given Fawad's background and the challenges he has faced, he's able to understand what's important in life. He is just as determined as anyone else to be the best he can be, but he also sees the bigger picture, and he seems able to have a positive attitude no matter what happens.

I'll always remember commentating a Big Bash game with Mark Waugh where Fawad was playing. Fawad was batting and we were saying that he really needed to accelerate the run rate. We suggested that Fawad should get off strike to get the other batter on strike as we thought it unlikely that he would be able to hit the ball to or over the rope. It was as though he heard us because he immediately proceeded to hit three sixes in a row. Later, Fawad uploaded on social media the footage of himself hitting those sixes with our commentary and some smiley emojis over it. We were so happy to be proven wrong by such a lovely guy and a great cricketer.

PLAYING CAREER

*as of 18 July, 2021

CAREER: 2013–present Australia; 2005–2010 Pakistan
MATCHES: 3 ODI, 3 T20I, 62 First Class
WICKETS: 3 ODI Wickets, 3 T20I Wickets, 205 FC Wickets
BOWLING AVERAGE: 48.33 ODI, 22.66 T20I, 31.11 FC average
BEST HAUL: 1/39 ODI, 3/25 T20I, 8/89 FC
BATTING: 4 ODI runs, 3 T20I runs, 410 FC runs
BATTING AVERAGE: 10.78 FC (ODI & T20I n/a)
FIELDING: 0 ODI & T20I dismissals

NATHAN LYON

An accidental superstar. Nathan Lyon went from cutting the grass at Adelaide Oval to picking up wickets and winning Australia Test matches on that same ground.

**BORN 20 NOVEMBER 1987
YOUNG, NEW SOUTH WALES**

NATHAN LYON

RIGHT-ARM OFF-SPIN BOWLER

Nathan Lyon was at the back of a group of spin bowlers being looked at to try to find a replacement for Shane Warne. It's not easy to replace the greatest leg-spin bowler of all time and there were certainly some casualties in the search. Though he's an off-spin bowler, not a leg-spin bowler, he was consistently good enough to keep getting picked.

Lyon took a wicket with the very first ball he bowled in Test cricket against one of the best batters in the world at that time, Kumar Sangakkara from Sri Lanka. He ended up taking five wickets in that first Test match bowling innings.

After an impressive Test debut, Nathan's career did not take off easily. He needed grit and determination to do the hard work needed to improve and stay at the top of his game. He had to work really hard to keep at it. It's a test of character and will to do that when you're faced with long, hard days of toil. It's a credit to Nathan that he has become the second leading Test wicket taker as a spin bowler for Australia and the greatest off-spinner that we've ever had.

It's important to remember how Nathan started, too. He worked as part of the grounds maintenance crew at Adelaide Oval. He has talked about how doing that job and being on the ground motivated him to practise more and dream about playing Test cricket for Australia.

It's no surprise that perhaps his most iconic performance in Test cricket was at the Adelaide Oval. It was a Test match against India in the summer of 2014. It was the first Test match after the sad passing of his good mate Phillip Hughes. It was an incredibly emotional game. Lyon came out and bowled Australia to victory in that Test match. He picked up seven wickets and led Australia to victory on the last day of the Test. It was a huge achievement, especially with all the emotion everyone was feeling. His finest cricketing moment came on the ground where he once cut the grass and mended the fences. He honoured his friend and made his country proud.

Nathan is also the appointed leader of the Australian Test team song, which is performed after the team's victories. He was chosen for this role for his great passion, skill, commitment and character shown when representing the Test team.

At heart, Nathan is still just a kid from country New South Wales – his values and down-to-earth character have never changed. Lyon has such an unassuming manner that somehow he seemed to sneak up and became the best performing statistically off-spin bowler for Australia. As soon as someone in the press labelled him GOAT (Greatest of All Time), it didn't take long for his teammates to jump on the nickname. And they're not wrong to call him that.

PLAYING CAREER

*as of 18 July, 2021

CAREER: 2011–present Test, 2012–2019 ODI
MATCHES: 100 Test, 29 ODI
WICKETS: 399 Test wickets, 29 ODI wickets
WICKETS IN AN INNINGS & MATCH: 18 five w/inns, 3 ten w/inns Test
BOWLING AVERAGE: 32.12 Test, 46.00 ODI
BEST HAUL: 8/50 Test, 4/44 ODI
BATTING: 1,101 Test runs, 77 ODI runs
BATTING AVERAGE: 12.23 Test, 19.25 ODI
FIELDING: 50 Test dismissals (50 Ct), 7 ODI dismissals (7 Ct)

ASHTON AGAR

One of the greatest debuts in Test history. This young man scored 98 batting at number 11. And he'd been selected as a bowler!

**BORN 14 OCTOBER 1993
MELBOURNE, VICTORIA**

ASHTON AGAR

LEFT-HANDED SPIN BOWLER

Ashton Agar rose to fame overnight. He was plucked out of almost obscurity to go on an Ashes tour in 2013. He debuted in Test cricket as a left arm orthodox spinner. He batted at number 11. He was dismissed for 98 on Test debut – it was so close to that 100 but what an incredible result and story. Imagine that – scoring 98 on debut at number 11 playing for Australia!

Having a support network around you is a great help when you're starting your career, especially when you're a very young player. Ashton has said that he looks up to his two younger brothers. He remembers many hours of backyard cricket with them and his dad as a kid. His mum has also been incredibly supportive. Ashton was called up to go on the Ashes tour so late that his parents only just made it to his baggy green presentation from Glenn McGrath. He describes that Test as one of the greatest experiences of his life. It means a lot when your biggest supporters can share your success with you.

It was tough for Agar to be thrust into the spotlight while he was so young and developing as a player. To be learning your game while playing cricket at the highest level is asking a lot of anyone. Ashton has said that it took him a while to work out how to deal with the pressure and the attention on him that came after his Test debut. He has been really open and honest about some mental health challenges he's had and about the mental aspect of the game. He has had to learn to deal with those challenges and the way he has talked about them no doubt helps others experiencing similar issues. I admire him greatly for his honesty and openness about these issues.

Ashton trains and works incredibly hard. He watches players he admires closely and tries to be like them or at least improve on his skills. Practising a skill so much that it becomes second nature can mean you are able to execute that skill perfectly when you're under pressure. Agar is clearly enjoying playing the game and it's beautiful to watch him develop.

Agar is another example of a versatile and skilled player of the modern game. I think he definitely has more Test cricket in his future, but he's developed into an extremely skilled and sought after One Day and T20 player. His batting, his bowling and his fielding is the absolute prototype for limited overs cricket. I love watching him play. The tricky thing with his schedule means he's not as prominently placed in front of selectors for Test selection. But after that debut his time with red-ball cricket will surely come again.

PLAYING CAREER
*as of 18 July, 2021

CAREER: 2013-present Test, 2015-present ODI, 2016-present T20I
MATCHES: 4 Test, 14 ODI, 34 T20I
WICKETS: 9 Test Wickets, 12 ODI Wickets, 39 T20I Wickets
WICKETS IN AN INNINGS & MATCH: 2 five w/inns T20I
BOWLING AVERAGE: 45.55 Test, 55.25 ODI, 20.48 T20I
BEST HAUL: 3/46 Test, 2/44 ODI, 6/30 T20I
BATTING: 195 Test runs, 217 ODI runs, 178 T20I runs
BATTING AVERAGE: 32.50 Test, 21.70 ODI, 11.86 T20I
FIELDING: 7 ODI dismissals (7 Ct), 21 T20I dismissals (21 Ct)

ASHLEIGH GARDNER

Ashleigh is a remarkable player. Not only is she out there playing for herself and her team, but she's also proudly representing her heritage.

**BORN 15 APRIL 1997
BANKSTOWN, NEW SOUTH WALES**

ASHLEIGH GARDNER

RIGHT-ARM OFF BREAK BOWLER

Ashleigh Gardner is one of just three First Nations players to play Test cricket for Australia, following Faith Thomas, who debuted in Test cricket in 1958, and Jason Gillespie, who debuted in Test cricket in 1996. Cricket has lagged behind other sports in Australia when it comes to participation levels among First Nations communities, but hopefully thanks to players like Ashleigh we will see that change and soon.

People coming into a sport can face similar challenges around developing their skills, working hard, sustaining their fitness, and managing the psychological side of playing elite sport. It has always interested me to see how players manage these things and then to find themselves representing a cultural or religious group on top of all that. Ashleigh's mother comes from the Muruwari people and Ashleigh is incredibly proud of her heritage. She's so thoughtful and considered in how she tries to make positive changes to the game. She is a role model.

Gardner's batting is so exciting to watch and truly reflective of the modern game. Every ball in Twenty20 cricket is a premium that you need to cash in on. Ashleigh has the fundamentals right, but she has worked on a power game as well. She has such impact in a match. She can go in and, in the space of 15 or 20 deliveries, she can completely change a game. She gets in and lifts the scoring rate and scores strike rates of 130 plus – more than a run a ball. She also bowls pretty handy off breaks as well, which never hurts. Her cricket is so exciting to watch and offers so much entertainment to fans.

A great moment in Ashleigh's career came against India in Melbourne at Junction Oval in February 2020. She got 93 from 57 deliveries. It was an innings that showed everyone that she could have a huge influence in short stints. Since then, she has started doing exactly that quite consistently.

Gardner's impact on an individual game is remarkable. But what's more impressive is the impact she is making on the sport. She is a an inspiration, and I look forward to seeing a lot more from her.

PLAYING CAREER

*as of 18 July, 2021

CAREER: 2017–present ODI & T20I
MATCHES: 36 ODI, 46 T20I
WICKETS: 42 ODI wickets, 23 T20I wickets
BOWLING AVERAGE: 25.73 ODI, 24.21 T20I
BEST HAUL: 3/28 ODI, 3/22 T20I
BATTING: 449 ODI runs, 812 T20I runs
BATTING AVERAGE: 22.45 ODI, 23.91 T20I
FIELDING: 16 ODI dismissals (16 Ct), 13 T20I dismissals (13 Ct)

STEVE WAUGH

An icon. It was an honour to play in a team with Steve Waugh as captain. He'll always be remembered as one of the greatest in Australian cricket.

**BORN 2 JUNE 1965
CANTERBURY, NEW SOUTH WALES**

STEVE WAUGH

RIGHT-HANDED ALLROUNDER

In my first call-up to the Australian team I was flown to India at short notice to replace Ian Healy, who was injured. I arrived at midnight and walked into the hotel room to meet my roommate ... and it was Steve Waugh! My hero. But he quickly fell in my estimation when I saw how messy the room was; it turns out he's disgracefully untidy!

But my first memory of Steve was when my older brother, Dean, was playing in regional NSW under 19s and Steve Waugh was dominating the game. He was so clearly way above and beyond all his peers, and I remember watching him and thinking how extraordinary he was. It felt like shortly after that he was playing Test cricket. In fact, Steve played his first Test in the 1985–86 season after his debut with NSW in 1984–85.

Being the most talented young player must have been a burden for Steve, but he carried it well. I'm sure people compared him to Donald Bradman, and the weight of expectation on him must have been so high. But it is amazing that pressure never seemed to make him second guess or doubt himself. It's important to remember that Steve started playing International cricket when Australia was pretty down and out. He was a huge part of turning that around. Bob Simpson was coaching and the younger players coming in had to work so hard to achieve the results the coaches and team desired. Fortunately, hard work is right up Steve's alley, and he helped lead the resurgence in Australian cricket.

Waugh was such an inspirational leader. It was clear he was always thinking about the team and how we could be successful as a group and as individuals. He challenged the team to do better always, and that's what good leaders need to do. He put in a huge amount of work and he expected those around him to do the same. He is a man of few words so that when he does speak, everyone listens and listens closely. He believed in and trusted his players. And that made us all lift to match his belief in us. He gave me an opportunity to bat top of the order in One Day cricket, which made me believe in my own capabilities a great deal more. It also put me in front of selectors so that when an opportunity to play Test cricket came up, I was on their minds. I have Steve to thank for that. That's the kind of person he is – inspiring others, getting them opportunities, keeping everyone working hard with their eye on the prize.

The tradition in Test cricket is if you win the toss, you bat first. The theory is you get runs on the board and the wicket is going to get worn out over the five days, so you don't want to be batting last. Steve flipped that to us as a challenge to the team. He looked at the conditions, but he believed we had the bowlers who could get the job done and then the batters who could bat big. He believed we were good enough to change it up and buck tradition. And that was just unheard of at that time. It was a new tactic and Steve led the way.

PLAYING CAREER

CAREER: 1985–2004 Test, 1886–2002 ODI
MATCHES: 168 Tests, 325 ODIs
RUNS: 10,927 Test runs, 7,569 ODI runs
CENTURIES & FIFTIES: 32 & 50 Test, 3 & 45 ODI
BATTING AVERAGE: 51.06 Test, 32.90 ODI
HIGH SCORE: 200 Test, 120* ODI
FIELDING: 112 Test dismissals (112 Ct), 111 ODI dismissals (111 Ct)

ALEX BLACKWELL

A pioneer of women's cricket. Alex was right in the middle of the movement that drew attention to women's cricket and made it the blockbuster game it is today.

**BORN 31 AUGUST 1983
WAGGA WAGGA, NEW SOUTH WALES**

ALEX BLACKWELL

RIGHT-HANDED ALLROUNDER

Alex Blackwell was not just a brilliant player of the game, she was also an inspiring captain and coach. At the same time that Alex was playing the game and fighting to get the recognition she and the sport deserved, she was also working hard at a grassroots level coaching young girls in junior cricket. This sums up who Alex is, and how she approaches cricket. She was always happy to get her hands dirty and lead by example, and she's incredibly motivational and engaged. I got to see this firsthand when Alex coached my young nieces. She instilled so much self-belief in them as well as teaching them the necessary skills and techniques. She made them love the game the way I do, which was a joy to see develop. I have no doubt that many of the professional women playing today were inspired to do so by Alex.

Blackwell was at the forefront of every aspect of the women's Big Bash League. So it was fitting that she was captain when her team Sydney Thunder won it in 2015–16. Blackwell saw opportunities for women's cricket and did everything she could to make them happen. It takes a special kind of person to do that.

Blackwell represented Australia in more than 250 matches and had a long and wonderful career. I remember noticing that her name was always on the team sheet. Her long consistent career had a very steadying influence. Blackwell made her international debut in 2003. Her batting skills were always powerful and precise, as reflected in her score of 100 in a One Day International. She played in 12 Tests, 144 One Day International matches and 95 T20 Internationals. She was also playing through the period of change in women's cricket, when it went from more traditional styles to the style we see today with the likes of Beth Mooney and Alyssa Healy. Towards the end of her career, Blackwell kept things steady and calm while the younger players she inspired to join the game in the first place pushed the limits even further.

Blackwell's involvement in cricket didn't end when she retired from playing. Her commitment to the game is obvious and her legacy will see women's cricket continue going from strength to strength. She has a tremendous knowledge and understanding of cricket and all the various partnerships and relationships that come with a broader cricketing landscape. She's a great facilitator of those relationships. Alex has a bright future ahead as a commentator and administrator of the sport.

PLAYING CAREER

CAREER: 2013–2017 Test & ODI, 2005–2017 T20I
MATCHES: 12 Tests, 144 ODIs, 96 T20Is
RUNS: 444 Test runs, 3,492 ODI runs, 1,314 T20I runs
CENTURIES & FIFTIES: 0 & 4 Test, 3 & 25 ODI, 0 & 1 T20I
WICKETS: 6 ODI Wickets
HIGH SCORE: 74 Test, 114 ODI
BEST HAUL: 2/8 ODI
BOWLING AVERAGE: 10.50 ODI
FIELDING: 6 Test dismissals (6 Ct), 55 ODI dismissals (55 Ct), 33 T20I dismissals (33 Ct)

MITCH MARSH

He's a terrific character with extraordinary natural talent and skills to play all aspects of the game, in any format. Whichever team you're on, you'll want Mitch Marsh to join you.

**BORN 20 OCTOBER 1991
PERTH, WESTERN AUSTRALIA**

MITCH MARSH

RIGHT-HANDED ALLROUNDER

We almost lost Mitch Marsh to AFL. Marsh is one of those super talented sportspeople who are multi-skilled across various codes. But thankfully for us, the cricket world was where he belonged. He shares his natural abilities with his father Geoff and brother Shaun, who both played Test cricket for Australia. I'm so glad he chose cricket over footy!

Marsh has the skills to play every aspect of the game. Since he dominated junior cricket from a young age, expectations of him have always been high. He can bat in the top order, he can open the bowling, and his catching is as good as anyone's. When he's fit and firing, he is a devastatingly impressive all-round cricketer. He's so versatile and can play many roles in a team as well as being able to play well across all modern formats of the game.

Since his Test debut, Marsh has become a regular selection for Australia in all three formats. His ability to hold his own with both bat and ball has been shown to give Australia an edge in close games, such as when he scored his maiden international century against India in a One Day International in 2016. Selection committees often see the true value of a player like Mitch Marsh which may not always be obvious if you only look at stats. He brings so much to a team and his versatility and skills are highly valued.

Marsh's breakthrough moment in Test cricket was when he scored 100 at the WACA. Scoring 100 in a Test match is a big moment in any cricketer's career but it's also a big moment for their family and friends and all the people who supported them to reach that milestone. It makes you reflect on all the time, sacrifices and support they have given you over the years. You don't achieve something like that without help and support. Mitch's 100 was a big moment for many of us.. I feel like I have been on Mitch's cricket journey with him as I've known him since he was a little boy running around the change rooms when I played with his dad. It's always so wonderful to see young people develop their skills and achieve their goals.

I think Mitch could play a big role in any of the three Australian teams for a few more years yet. We'll be seeing plenty more of him in Test, One Day and T20 formats. His natural abilities and strength will hold him in good stead. He's such a dominating player that if he can avoid injuries and stay fit, he'll have a big role to play.

PLAYING CAREER

*as of 18 July, 2021

CAREER: 2014-present Test, 2011-present ODI & T20I
MATCHES: 32 Tests, 60 ODIs, 25 T20I
RUNS: 1,260 Test Runs, 1,615 ODI Runs, 544 T20I Runs
CENTURIES & FIFTIES: 2 & 3 Test, 1 & 12 ODI
WICKETS: 42 Test Wickets, 49 ODI Wickets, 15 T20I Wickets
WICKETS IN AN INNINGS & MATCH: 1 five w/inns Test, 1 five w/inns ODI
BATTING AVERAGE: 25.20 Test, 34.36 ODI, 27.20 T20I
BOWLING AVERAGE: 38.64 Test, 36.79 ODI, 16.46 T20I
BEST HAUL: 5/46 Test, 5/33 ODI, 2/6 T20I
FIELDING: 16 Test dismissals (16 Ct), 28 ODI dismissals (28 Ct), 9 T20I dismissals (9 Ct)

ANDREW SYMONDS

What a character!
One of my favourites to play with.
I would have him in any cricket
team that I could play in.

**BORN 9 JUNE 1975
BIRMINGHAM, ENGLAND**

ANDREW SYMONDS

RIGHT-HANDED ALLROUNDER

Playing with Andrew Symonds was a highlight of my career. He is the most laid-back person who had completely natural abilities. He trained incredibly hard and always brought everything he had onto the field, but he did not want to think about cricket outside of that. He knew that if he thought about it too much, his mind would get tangled and it would affect his performance. So he enjoyed his downtime and could really relax.

If you could make the ideal cricketer for all three versions of the game in a computer lab, it would make Symonds. His batting skill was made for T20 cricket. He had power, he could hit sixes, he could score as quick a rate as anyone. He could bowl and had true versatility in his bowling, ranging from medium pace to spin depending on the conditions and his opponent. He is in the top five fielders that I have ever seen. His reflexes were just amazing and you could really rely on his throwing arm. And on top of all that skill and versatility, his athleticism and strength were first-class. He was a true three-dimensional cricketer.

I'll always remember the first game in the Cricket World Cup in 2003. We played Pakistan in Johannesburg. The night before the first game, we learned that Shane Warne had been suspended and would not be playing. We could feel the focus of the cricketing world on us. We tried to remain focused on the game but found ourselves in a real pressure situation. Symonds came out and scored 140, totally saving the innings and putting us in a position where we could go on and win the game. We went on and won the World Cup undefeated. There are pivotal moments in a series and it's unusual that they come so early. But had Symonds not stood up and put in that extraordinary performance, anything could have happened. He filled us with confidence and it was one of his most valuable contributions when we needed him most.

Symonds got into his fair share of trouble and was disciplined regularly in his career. He was incredibly competitive on the field and did not shy away from conflict. Off the field, his carefree attitude led to him being a little reckless at times. He's a fine example of the importance of learning how to balance the off-field lifestyle of a professional athlete with the on-field responsibilities.

For Symonds, the team was everything. When he made mistakes, he was very hard on himself and upset that he let the team down. Symonds was a fiercely loyal teammate. He had strong values and believed that we all had to do whatever we could for each other. He faced a lot of racism in his cricketing career and I wish more had been done to support him through that. Loyalty was so important to Symonds and he rightly felt let down. I hope it's something we will never see or hear on the cricket pitch again.

PLAYING CAREER

CAREER: 2004-2008 Test, 1998-2009 ODI, 2005-2009 T20I
MATCHES: 26 Tests, 198 ODIs, 14 T20Is
RUNS: 1,462 Test runs, 5,088 ODI runs, 337 T20I runs
CENTURIES & FIFTIES: 2 & 10 Test, 6 & 30 ODI, 0 & 2 T20I
HIGH SCORE: 162* Test, 156 ODI, 85* T20I
WICKETS: 24 Test wickets, 133 ODI wickets, 8 T20I wickets
WICKETS IN AN INNINGS & MATCH: 1 five w/inns ODI
BEST HAUL: 3/50 Test, 5/18 ODI, 2/14 T20I
BOWLING AVERAGE: 37.33 Test, 37.25 ODI, 34.62 T20I
FIELDING: 22 Test Dismissals (22 Ct), 82 ODI dismissals (82 Ct), 3 T20I dismissals (3 Ct)

ELLYSE PERRY

Ellyse is one of her generation's great pioneering players. She brought a new skill level and a new audience to the game.

**BORN 3 NOVEMBER 1990
SYDNEY, NEW SOUTH WALES**

ELLYSE PERRY

RIGHT-HANDED ALLROUNDER

There is nothing Ellyse Perry can't do. She's that good. And not just at cricket. Ellyse has represented Australia in both cricket and soccer World Cups. She became the youngest Australian ever to play senior international cricket when she debuted in Darwin in July 2007 at just sixteen years old. She's one of the most versatile sportspeople we've seen for a long time. She scored a goal in the women's World Cup football tournament and then scored a Test match double century. That's a pretty rare feat.

Ellyse is a phenomenally talented cricketer. She worked so hard to hone her skills and maintain a high fitness level. She was the best in the game for a significant amount of time. She has remained so humble and balanced and has a great perspective on everything about life and about sport and where it all fits in. Ellyse is truly the complete package cricketer and she has skill, endurance, charisma and finesse. She's a total allrounder who bats right-handed and bowls right-arm pace. Her fielding is second to none and she has a very strong throwing arm. On top of all that, she's a kind and humble person.

Ellyse started playing so young. That was at a time when it was common for female cricketers to be pushed up a level when they were still quite young. As the game has progressed and more professional pathways have been developed, that has changed.

I remember Australia played India in a women's game at the MCG before we played England that night in the men's game. I watched Ellyse pick up five wickets. She was only 16 or 17 years old and I was amazed at how calm and composed she was. She could easily have let the enormity of the moment get the better of her, but she just stayed cool and calm. She hardly even celebrated the wickets. She was so focused and determined, and I knew then she was destined for greatness. Her composure combined with her skills and athleticism made everyone pay attention.

Ellyse has done so much to draw attention to women's cricket both from fans and the media. Everything she has done has raised the profile of the sport. I have no doubt that many of the young girls playing cricket today are doing so because Ellyse inspired them and showed them the way. In fact, she's probably playing with a few of them today. What a remarkable legacy to have made.

PLAYING CAREER

*as of 18 July, 2021

CAREER: 2008–present Test, 2007–present ODI, 2008–present T20I
MATCHES: 8 Tests, 115 ODIs, 123 T20I
RUNS: 624 Test Runs, 3,107 ODI Runs, 1,243 T20I Runs
CENTURIES & FIFTIES: 2 & 2 Test, 2 & 28 ODI, 0 & 4 T20I
WICKETS: 31 Test Wickets, 152 ODI Wickets, 115 T20I Wickets
BOWLING AVERAGE: 18.19 Test, 24.50 ODI, 19.27 T20I
WICKETS IN AN INNINGS & MATCH: 2 five w/inns Test, 3 five w/inns ODI
HIGH SCORE & BEST HAUL: 213* & 6/32 Test, 112* & 7/22 ODI, 60* & 4/12 T20I
BATTING AVERAGE: 78.00 Test, 51.78 ODI, 28.90 T20I
FIELDING: 5 Test dismissals (5 Ct), 38 ODI dismissals (38 Ct), 37 T20I dismissals (37 Ct)

CAMERON GREEN

*A rising star.
A shining beacon of hope
in the cricketing landscape.*

**BORN 3 JUNE 1999
SUBIACO, WESTERN AUSTRALIA**

CAMERON GREEN

RIGHT-HANDED ALLROUNDER

Cameron Green is tall. Really tall. And the expectations on him have always been high. He has been talked about as the best Australian batting talent since Ricky Ponting. That's a lot of pressure to sit on those shoulders. My hope for Cameron is that he can continue to rise to his full potential, even when he hits the inevitable speed bumps and setbacks that are part of any sportsperson's journey.

Cricket is Green's first love, though he could have chosen to have a career in AFL. I remember hearing Cameron's name for the first time when he was 12 years old. That's an early age to be singled out as a talent to watch. There are a lot of talented kids out there but they don't all make it to professional cricket careers, so it's a testament to Cameron that he has been able to follow his cricketing path to the top. He seems to take it all in his stride and doesn't show any signs of nervousness or panic. I have no doubt that in big pressure moments his heart is racing, but being able to hide your emotions from your opponent does give you an advantage at the top level of sport. Cameron always seems cool, calm and collected.

Where Cameron truly shines is his batting. Green is much taller than batters have traditionally been. Usually players as tall as Green would be bowlers. His batting technique is simple, technically correct and based on a strong foundation of defence. He follows a more traditional set-up in getting his defence right and then elaborating and expanding on that. This makes Cameron a bit of an outlier as a modern young cricketer. Many young cricketers are thinking about Twenty20 cricket, smashing sixes, throwing the textbook out and just swinging wildly.

Cameron can expand into this as he gains experience. But there is something to be said for using a foundation of defence to establish and build an innings. Green is not flamboyant in his batting technique or stroke play – he lets his skills do all the work. He's a disciplined batter and it's really nice to watch.

Cameron's batting has been the focus for the past two years, but he is also a skilled bowler. He picked up five wickets in his first game for Western Australia. Frustratingly, injury setbacks have meant he hasn't been able to truly show what he's capable of as a bowler. If he can get back to bowling, though, any cricket team will do anything to have a genuine allrounder like him.

PLAYING CAREER

*as of 18 July, 2021

CAREER: 2010-present Test, 2017-present FC
MATCHES: 4 Tests, 29 FC, 13 T20
RUNS: 236 Test, 2,116 FC, 106 T20
CENTURIES & FIFTIES: 0 & 1 Test, 7 & 4 FC
HIGH SCORE: 84 Test, 251 FC, 36 T20
WICKETS: 34 FC wickets
WICKETS IN AN INNINGS & MATCH: 2 five w/inns FC
BOWLING AVERAGE: 31.08 FC
BEST HAUL: 6/30 FC
FIELDING: 5 Test Dismissals (5 Ct), 13 FC dismissals (13 Ct)

ADAM GILCHRIST

Adam Gilchrist is one of Australia's best-known and best-loved cricketers in the game's history. 'Gilly' was a record-breaking wicketkeeper, outstanding left-hand batter and vice-captain of the Australian team.

Gilly's remarkable career as a wicketkeeper batter for Australia from 1996 to 2008 saw him set a new standard for wicketkeeping as well as collecting honours including a Wisden Cricketer of the Year (2002), the Allan Border medal (2003) and One Day International Player of the Year (2003 and 2004).

Gilchrist was a player that everyone wanted to watch. He was also known for his sporting conduct. He demonstrated exemplary integrity at the 2003 World Cup at Port Elizabeth where he 'walked' after he touched a ball but was given not out, a decision he held himself accountable for in matches thereafter.

Upon retiring from international cricket in 2008, Gilchrist played in the Indian Premier League for six seasons. He still keeps a keen eye on cricket in his role as commentator, in which he has the privilege of commenting on the next generation of cricketers – some of whom he's described in this book.

Loved by cricketers and cricket fans all over for his inspiring leadership, his honest reflections on the game and its players, and his respect and love for the game, Adam Gilchrist is a true champion of cricket.